"Oh, dear. I didn't even offer to help." Leah clasped her hands together, worry creasing her brow.

Mark reached out and caught her fingers. She jumped, almost pulling back before catching herself. Staring down to where he'd grabbed her hands, his darker ones covering her pale skin, she realized how long it had been since a man had actually held her hands.

"No reason to be nervous," he said. "That's a bad habit of yours, clasping your hands whenever you're worried.

She swallowed, reminding herself that Mark worked for the sheriff. As handsome and attractive as he was, she had to get a grip on herself. She couldn't let her guard down.

Forcing herself to relax, she smiled gently at Mark. "I'll remember that," she said.

Books by Cheryl Wolverton

Love Inspired

A Matter of Trust #11
A Father's Love #20
This Side of Paradise #38
The Best Christmas Ever #47
A Mother's Love #63
*For Love of Zach #76
*For Love of Hawk #87
*For Love of Mitch #105
*Healing Hearts #118
*A Husband To Hold #136

*Hill Creek, Texas

CHERYL WOLVERTON

grew up in a military town, though her father was no longer in the service when she was born. She attended Tomlinson Junior High School and Lawton High School, and was attending Cameron when she met her husband, Steve. After a whirlwind courtship of two weeks they became engaged. Four months later they were married, and that was over seventeen years ago.

Cheryl and Steve have two wonderful children, Christina, sixteen, and Jeremiah, thirteen. Cheryl loves having two teenagers in the house.

As for books, Cheryl has written nine novels for the Steeple Hill Love Inspired line and is currently working on new novels. You can contact Cheryl at P.O. Box 207, Slaughter, LA 70777. She loves to hear from readers.

A Husband To Hold
Cheryl Wolverton

Published by Steeple Hill Books™

STEEPLE HILL BOOKS

Steeple
Hill™

ISBN 0-373-87143-0

A HUSBAND TO HOLD

Copyright © 2001 by Cheryl Wolverton

This edition published by arrangement with Steeple Hill Books.

® and TM are trademarks of Steeple Hill Books, used under license. Trademarks indicated with ® are registered in the United States Patent and Trademark Office, the Canadian Trade Marks Office and in other countries.

Visit us at www.steeplehill.com

Printed in U.S.A.

For thou art my rock and my fortress;
therefore for Thy name's sake lead me, and guide me.
—*Psalms:* 31:3

Dedicated to my mother-in-law, Phyllis,
and my father-in-law, Mr. Wolverton, aka John.
Thanks for your wonderful son.
He's a rare treasure. Also to Dottie Ramsey,
one of the best teachers I've ever met.

Acknowledgments:

To the Zachary Police Department. My kids
have grown up with you guys and you're the best.
Thanks for the job you do and thanks
for being there to use in a purely fictional way.

Thanks also to my wonderful gentle editor,
Patience Smith, who takes time to tell me how she
feels about my stories, and works with me to help
me grow. You are a treasure, dear one, whom I hope
to have a long time! And to my agent, Deidre.
Thanks for representing me! And always to
my husband, Steve, and my kids, Christina and
Jeremiah (though if you are an English teacher at
Zachary High or Northwestern Middle,
you don't know they're my kids!).

Prologue

September, 1994

"Ashes to ashes. Dust to dust..."

Leah Hawkins heard the words as she stared at the casket before her. It was over, done with, finished.

She wanted to cry, but the tears would not come. She was still too much in shock over what she'd discovered about her husband only three days ago when the person had showed up at her door.

"...an honorable man who served as one of our city's finest..."

Honorable? She stared at the coffin as the preacher rambled on. She had thought her husband honorable. Everyone in church had thought him honorable. Otherwise he wouldn't have been a deacon. Even Zachary's finest had thought him honorable or he wouldn't have been a police officer.

"…commit him now to a heavenly father…"

Commit him to God? Leah could only hope God would have mercy on his soul. How she prayed God would have mercy. She hoped. She prayed, but she could not cry.

The horrible tales backed up with evidence told by the person on that awful day still filled her mind.

"…and we finally ask, Almighty God, that You find the murderer of this fine respected citizen, this loving husband and father, this upright Christian…"

Leah's heart beat faster. Looking down at her husband's still, peaceful face she thought, the pastor can pray for someone to find your murderer, Bobby, but I already know who murdered you.

She knew. And so did one other person.

Glancing up, her gaze riveted to the man standing at the opposite end of the procession. He was a man in uniform, wearing gloves, teary eyed and in mourning with the others around him. A pallbearer, he was well-known himself. The press had interviewed him about her husband's death. They had no details, except he'd been killed in the line of duty. The murderer had covered all tracks well, except for one small detail.

One person besides her knew who the murderer was.

Her husband's partner.

Dan Milano.

She had proof of the murder.

And he suspected it.

What would he do? Would he come after her for that proof? Put out a warrant? There was no telling what would happen. She knew how police officers worked. And she couldn't stick around to find out if Dan would pursue her in this very deadly game.

She knew, when the funeral was over, she would never be safe here in Zachary again. Or anywhere else in Louisiana for that matter. She would have to walk away from this funeral, away from her life, away from everything she had or risk exposing the truth, the secret she held. A secret that could very well lead to her death.

Chapter One

Present Day

"I hear you're interested in learning a bit more about our countryside?"

Leah Thomas looked up from the box of papers she was going through. Glancing across the room to locate the librarian and anyone else browsing the aisles, she sized up the man in front of her.

Tall, slender, dark hair and dark good looks with a slightly Cajun accent, he leaned casually against the card file cabinet, his arms and sneakered feet crossed.

"You're Laura's brother," Leah commented, placing him from church. Laura Walker McCade had come to Hill Creek, Texas, a few years before, intent on finding this missing brother, only to end up having amnesia and nearly being killed. It had taken Zach's help and Laura's need to know to finally locate Mark, who had been hiding out from a local drug ring. Mark had actually been helping the FBI, if the rumors were true.

Leah shivered with memory.

"That's me, *chérie*," he drawled and Leah well knew he was saying *dear* in that Cajun French of his. She'd heard all about the cowboy who spoke French. She could point him out as well. Any single female—and a few married ones—could.

"My sister sent me over here to talk with you," he continued. "She's busy with her new baby son and stepdaughter and couldn't take you up on your idea but thought I'd be ideal for the job."

Dressed in dark blue jeans and a light-blue button-down shirt, this man looked as if he could handle anything. Broad shoulders, lean hips, a cocky smile. But...

"You work for Sheriff Mitch McCade," she murmured.

"I am the official photographer and *basically* work for him. It's more of a contractual type thing," Mark Walker corrected. "Is that a problem?"

Dropping the papers back into the box, she shook her head. "I don't—of course not."

She smoothed the light pink, granny-style dress she wore and then shoved her blond hair back behind her ear. Knowing her nervous conduct wasn't lost on this man she winced inwardly. Still, she couldn't help her reactions. "I really just need to learn how to do some photography for a class I'm going to be leading into the wilderness later this summer break. That, and I need to find a few good camping spots. I suppose I could do that on my own, Mr. Walker, since Laura isn't available. I mean, I did ask her months ago."

Mark pushed away from the catalogue file he leaned against and removed the toothpick from his mouth.

Leah couldn't help but tense.

"Really now, Ms. Thomas, I don't mind at all. I know you're a favorite of the kids over there at school. And believe me, with all of Freckles McCade's family out where I live, I have a feeling this would be a much needed break from the noise."

Leah relaxed hearing him mention Dr. Julian McCade's wife, Susan, and her brothers and sisters, who lived out on an old farm with them. "That's right. Sherri mentioned you live out there in a converted bunkhouse."

"Freckles's sister? Yeah. She would mention that." Grinning a sardonic grin he strolled over and lowered himself to one of the four chairs that were set around the table where Leah's research box sat. "So, why don't you tell me a little bit about what you'd like to learn?"

Leah hesitated. She didn't care overly much for the police but as long as Laura and Mark had been in town she'd learned they were good citizens and nice people—at least on the outside. Even if they were good people, she still had to worry about letting something slip or being recognized. But this program meant so much to her.

Sitting at a right angle to him, she resigned herself to talking with this man. "We are having a tri-county special session for the exceptional children in the area. I've managed to get a small grant that will partially pay for thirteen handicapped children to go on a nature expedition. It's to enrich their learning experiences and social interaction."

Mark nodded, slipping the toothpick back in his mouth. "I heard something about this. Jon mentioned it in the pulpit the other day," he said, referring to their pastor, Jon Ferguson.

"Yes. He did. Pastor Ferguson has been instrumental in getting the word out about the summer opportunity for these handicapped children."

"So what exactly do you need?" Mark asked now.

"Well," Leah began. If there was one thing that

could overcome her wariness toward others, it was the discussion of children. Not six weeks after her husband's death she lost her own child in a miscarriage. She still grieved over the loss of her unborn child and her husband. The children that she taught almost filled that empty spot that had never completely healed. No matter how she cried out to God over her loss there was still a part of her that grieved, one little area where she had hidden the past.

She had a feeling she'd never stop grieving her child's loss or her husband's death until the chapter of her former life closed.

But solving the past would never happen. She wouldn't and couldn't let it happen. She was safe here, living again. She threw herself into helping these kids here at Hill Creek to take her mind off that emptiness, refusing to trust any person completely except her children. Smiling now as she talked about "her" children, she said, "The places I am going to take them have to be mapped out before I get final approval. I already have the adult supervisors and equipment. The only other paraphernalia I need are simply the things the state of Texas wants for publicity and such."

"So you want...?" Mark asked.

"I want a guide to help me map out a safe route for a two-night stay in the desert. I want the guide to teach me how to use a camera and help me take some photographs of the area for this mission. And I'm willing to pay.''

Mark Walker studied the petite blonde before him. Though Leah may have acted as if she needed time to place him, he hadn't required a moment to identify who she was. His first day in church he'd noticed her.

She was gentle, so very feminine, quiet—how could he not notice her? The way she shied away from Mitch and his sister, Laura, made the sheriff keep an eye on her.

She reminded him of an injured wren that needed protecting. Whether Leah knew it or not, half the town watched out for her. He knew Mitch certainly did. Mitch had actually thought of marrying this woman at one time when he'd been looking for someone to settle down with. Of course, Mitch had almost married every woman in town so that didn't really count.

He was glad when Suzi had snagged Mitch. The man had been totally blind to the fact Suzi loved him.

Leah would have never done for Mitch. She was high maintenance, he'd bet anything. Looking at the wide blue eyes now as she stared up at him, Mark would wager the woman wouldn't know how to get on a bus and travel to the next town without help.

Not that she was ignorant, just...helpless.

Exactly the type of woman Mark didn't want. He didn't want someone who would pin him down, nor did he want someone who would hem him in. He was free of his past life, of his father's wishes that he be a police officer. Of his sister's mothering. He wanted to do what *he* wanted to do—although he still wasn't sure what that was.

But it would be what he wanted to do. And this job that the young woman had just mentioned certainly sounded right up his alley. A slight tug of conscience reminded him of his job as deputy but he evaded it, concentrating instead on his favorite hobby—photography and exploration of the surrounding area.

He wouldn't mind helping her for a short time. Leah was certainly easy on the eyes. And she was a Christian, with Christian attitudes. She was also simply a gentle kind woman who needed help.

"So, how much are you paying?" he asked, smiling now at her.

She named an amount.

Eyebrows going up, he reached up and pulled the toothpick from his mouth. "*Chérie,* that is quite a bit of money. Are you sure you have your figures right?"

Leah gripped her hands together indecisively. "Actually, you see, that's part of the money I was allotted in the proposal I worked up for the grant. I had to write out where the money would be used. I told them I would have someone mapping out a section of the safest handicapped-accessible routes and that her or his time would run that much."

Surprised, Mark reevaluated the woman. "You have all of your facts pretty well laid out, I see," he murmured.

The pale skin of her cheeks flushed a light pink. "I try to be prepared in everything and for any eventuality."

Mark cocked his head studying her. "That sounds so ominous, *chérie*. Are you expecting a tornado or hailstorm while we're out on the range?"

Leah laughed and shook her head before reaching up and pushing her hair back behind her ear. "No. No. I just meant, it's good to be prepared. Especially where children are concerned. You can never be too careful."

A soft pang of hurt echoed in her voice. He doubted she even realized she'd revealed that. Caught up in her vulnerability, he thought this is what always got him in trouble. Don't worry about it, Mark, he warned himself. It's your imagination.

"I'll be glad to take the job," he found himself saying.

However, it wasn't for the job's sake that he'd agreed, he realized, but to get to know this woman better.

Leah's face brightened though a fleeting shadow of doubt touched her eyes. "Great! Then can we meet Monday to go over what I have planned for the camp-out?"

He should run now, not note how appealing the offer was. But it was too late. He'd been absorbed in her enthusiasm and fleeting hints of a deeper character within her. He wouldn't back off now. No, he'd go for it.

How hard could it be after all? He'd simply hold her hand and walk her through what she wanted to know and then be done with it.

"Sounds good to me, *chérie*," he murmured.

"Great!" Clapping her hands she smiled, a beautiful full smile of pleasure, and Mark suddenly wondered if he was setting himself up for something he was going to regret.

Chapter Two

It might be harder than he had thought, Mark mused, unnerved by the look on Sheriff Mitch McCade's face as they stood in the middle of the main office.

"You're doing what?"

Mitch McCade stared, slack-jawed at Mark.

"I said I'm going to need a leave of absence for a short time to map out the local areas...if that's okay with you." Mark shifted, cocking a hip as he waited for Mitch to answer.

Mitch slowly shook his head. "No, it's not, Mark. You said you were taking Leah Thomas to map out the local areas."

Every sound in the sheriff's office died. Mark knew why. Every person had stopped to listen to the exchange between the two men. Mark scowled at his boss. "She needs someone to help her. And she's *paying* me. It's just a job."

Mitch snorted. "It was the eyes, wasn't it?"

"Mitch McCade!" Assistant Deputy Laura McCade, Mitch's sister-in-law, yelled loud enough and with enough reproach to make Mitch flush and the entire office break into chuckles.

Glaring at his sister-in-law, Mitch said, "Stay out of it, Laura, or I'll tell them all how you really ended up going into labor."

Mark glanced over at Laura, who had turned the color of a rosy sunset. "Yeah, Sis, stay out of it."

"Zach is going to hear about this," she muttered good-naturedly.

"He's my big brother but *not* my keeper," Mitch said casually, smiling. Then he turned his attention back to the man in front of him. "Come with me, to my office."

Mark nodded and followed his boss down the short, dark, narrow hallway. At twenty-nine, Mark was younger than Mitch McCade. The brawny man with the dark skin and hair spoke Spanish almost as well as a native speaker. After breaking a drug ring and discovering his former deputy sheriff had been the one running it in their area, Mitch hired his sister-in-law, Laura, the big-city detective, to assist him in the office.

Laura had finagled a job for her brother Mark.

Mark liked the job except for one small detail: it was what his father expected of him. After the way his father had raised them, Mark wanted nothing to do with that type of life. The memories were too harsh, too cold. His father had never been home and had been what was known as a hardnose both with work and with his family.

Still, Mark couldn't help but hang around the Hill Creek County Sheriff's Department since it seemed he had a natural knack for this sort of thing. Their boots echoed as they walked down the cracking linoleum floor.

Turning into Mitch's office, Mark paused to close the door then dropped into a chair in front of the old wooden desk. It had been scratched up, used, abused, but still stood. Mark wouldn't be surprised to find this was still the original desk from when this building had been built back in the late 1800s.

Mitch strode around his desk and sat down. Leaning back, he propped his feet up on the desk. Crossing his hands over his flat abdomen he said, "So, tell me what's going on, Mark?"

Mark tossed his toothpick into the nearby dented metal receptacle and pulled out a small bottle from his pocket. Snagging a fresh toothpick, he slid it into his mouth before replacing the container within the confines of the material. ''You know Leah, Mitch. Laura said with her baby duties and her stepdaughter, Angela, starting college she didn't have the time to do a proper job of helping Leah out.''

When Mitch said nothing but continued to stare, Mark shifted in his chair and finally admitted, ''You know how my sister is. She poured it on really thick how we just couldn't let that poor fragile woman go out in the desert all alone, pointing out how many times I'd mentioned how helpless Leah Thomas looked.''

Mitch chuckled to Mark's everlasting frustration. ''She got to you, huh?''

''Just wait, Sheriff. My sister has been at me nearly thirty years. You, she only has been after a couple now.''

Mitch chuckled again.

''Besides, it was you she went with to the neighbor's house.''

Mitch stopped laughing. ''Yeah, well…your sister can certainly be sly when she wants to be. She was too far along to be running around like she did.''

Mark only smirked, not believing any of the story Mitch had. ''You see why I want the leave?''

Mitch dropped his feet and leaned forward, resting his forearms on a stack of papers that lay haphazardly across his desk. "Partially. Let me ask you something else though, Walker."

"Sure," Mark agreed. "Shoot."

Mitch studied him, his dark-brown eyes perusing every facet as if seeking a weakness or flaw. Mark didn't like it when men did that. But with Mitch it was downright unnerving how well he could pick out the problems.

"You still running from God about some issues?"

Mark sighed. Dropping his gaze, he again admitted that Mitch had hit the head of the nail dead-on. "What does that matter?"

Leaning back in his chair, Mitch again crossed his arms over his abdomen though he didn't prop up his booted feet this time. "If you're still rebelling against your dad's wishes out of pure stubbornness and using this as a way not to be around the job, yeah, it matters."

"Would I have taken the job in the first place if I felt that way?" Mark demanded.

Mitch met his gaze never flinching as he replied, "Yeah, you would because you are one of the best natural detectives I've ever seen. You crave this work but at the same time detest it for what it did to your family. Now, if you're going out to help Leah, that's one thing. But if you're simply vacillating again, then I'd suggest you not shortchange Leah that way."

"Mais, non!" Mark said lapsing into Cajun French. Jerking the toothpick out of his mouth, he continued, "You are my brother-in-law, Mitch McCade, but you do not know what it was like and I will not have you trying to probe my mind."

Mitch relaxed, a look of concern replacing his hardened flat gaze. "Listen, bro," he said softly, using a shortened version of the Christian term *brother,* something he often did. "I wouldn't ask if I weren't worried. I can't think of anyone I'd rather have on the team here. But your heart isn't in it. That can be dangerous. I'm worried about you. Laura is worried about you...."

"Are you going to fire me?" Mark asked, calming down and slowly forcing himself to relax.

Mitch snorted. "Yeah, right. When you're worth as much as you are—even part-time. The only way you're getting off this force is by quitting."

"Don't tempt me," Mark muttered. After slipping the toothpick back in his mouth, he folded his hands across his stomach. "I don't know what I want, Mitch." Rubbing his hand down his face, he admitted, "I don't know if I want to stay with this job or leave it."

"You know what, Mark?" Mitch grinned. "Maybe this is exactly what you need. Time with

Leah, who is so leery of police officials and men in general, will either convince you that you've got the right job or chase you away from it.''

"So many people come out here not wanting to talk about their past. She's one of them.'' He then continued, "She can be defensive all she wants. At least she's protecting herself that way.''

Mitch cocked his head curiously.

Mark remained passive, refusing to allow his brother-in-law to see just how much Leah had affected him. Still, when Mitch nodded, with that speculative look filling his features, Mark had to wonder if he'd blown his cover.

"I think you're right, Walker'' was all Mitch replied. "Remember though, while you're considering if you want this job, some people can simply walk away from it, but others are called. I think you're called to this job, Mark. It's in your blood and I don't think you can turn your back on it, regardless of what you think. However—'' pushing back from his desk, he stood "—six weeks' leave of absence is granted.''

Mark stared, stunned. He hadn't thought he would get that much when he'd requested it. He'd honestly thought Mitch would badger him into working half weeks or every other day.

"Six weeks,'' he repeated, echoing Mitch.

Mitch nodded. "Yeah. Six entire weeks. I hope

this is what you want and you'll take time to find your heart while you're out there, Mark. We'll all miss you, but I really think this is God in the working."

A spine-tingling sensation spread down Mark's back at those words.

God in the working.

Those words echoed eerily inside him and as much as he wanted to deny what Mitch had said, he knew God's ways were greater than his own ways.

"Whatever," he said instead. "Now, if you'll excuse me, I need to run by the hardware store and then go make sure Leah knows I'll be available starting tomorrow."

Mitch grinned. "You do that. And give her my regards, too."

Relieved the interrogation was over, Mark stood and strode toward the door. "You give your own regards, Mitch. I've got a job to do and that's all I plan to do."

Mitch's deep rich chuckle followed him out the room, taunting him to keep that pledge of "business only" as he faced the sweet, gentle soul named Leah Thomas.

Chapter Three

"I hear you might have found someone to help you out?" Tessa said.

Leah glanced up at her best friend after shoving a camera into her backpack. "I suppose so. How'd you hear about Laura's brother, though?"

Curiously she paused in the preparation of her knapsack to study the diminutive woman lounging on the couch, one leg lazily swinging back and forth over the arm of the cloth-covered sofa.

"The neighbor told me when I pulled up that Deputy Walker had been here the other day. I would think that was the only reason he'd be here, knowing how you like to keep to yourself."

Leah sighed, understanding when Tessa was simply pumping her for information and that her dear gossipy neighbor wanted her to talk. "Mrs. Mulching tells all, doesn't she?" Leah returned to stuffing her bag full of beef jerky, a full canteen and sunblock. She also tried to figure out just what to inform her dear friend Tessa.

Continuing to swing her leg as she reclined on the sofa, Tessa nodded, drawing Leah's attention back to her. "From what I've seen, she does tell all. So, if you have someone to go with you and help you, why don't you just wait and let him take you out to study the area instead of going on your own today?"

That was Tessa. She was pretty much to the point with Leah. Leah had obviously waited too long to tell her what she wanted to hear so she'd simply asked. Leah always knew where she stood with this woman. And Tessa hadn't mellowed one bit now that she was married. "Where is Drake?" she asked mildly, trying to change the subject.

Tessa chuckled, giving Leah a knowing look. Running her fingers through her short brown hair, she shifted on the sofa and crossed her legs. "With his therapist. His limp is almost gone. When he's done I'll pick him up and give him the books I borrowed from you. Then I get to bully him into reading some more for me."

Leah chuckled. Tessa's husband, Drake, had been through an awful ordeal only a few months

before. Many thought he wouldn't make it, but
he'd proven the town wrong. Systematically, day
by day, Drake had pulled himself from the brink
of death to where he was now. He'd met Tessa
who was reteaching him to read after the accident
that had caused so much damage. It had been love
at first sight. Rarely did Tessa make it over to chat
anymore. Except when something new was obviously in the air. Tessa seemed to feel so responsible for Leah.

She wondered if this concern was just natural
for Tessa or if it was because Leah tended to be
thought of as fragile by most people. "I can't believe he is up to poetry by Burns," Leah murmured
before zipping the bag up.

"He sure is. Now, why don't you answer my
question, dear, and tell me why you're on your way
out to the desert when you have a perfectly good
helper you're going to be paying to do the dirty
work for you?"

Leah lifted the bag and moved over across from
Tessa. Seating herself on the sofa, she dropped the
bag on her khaki-covered legs. Smoothing the pink
top, she paused to push a strand of blond hair behind her ear. "I am perfectly capable of handling
things myself, Tessa, and I can't believe you said
that," she said carefully.

Tessa dropped her feet to the floor and leaned

forward. "You know that's not what I meant at all. I know how capable you are."

Leah didn't believe that. Her face said otherwise.

"I meant, get your money's worth. Mark is a photographer and has been all over the area out there. Why not leave it to him and concentrate on the rest of the planning you have back here?"

Leah sighed. How did she explain that allowing another person to get close to her was not something she could accept? She'd thought she could, but in the end...

She couldn't say out loud that she was afraid, without revealing too much of herself.

"He doesn't know where I want the pictures. I thought I'd go out there and mark two or three of the areas I wanted, take some snapshots to give him ideas of the types of places I want and need, and then let him do the rest."

Tessa nodded slowly. "That does make sense.... But you do realize there are snakes out right now? They're especially bad this year."

Leah interlocked her fingers, clasping her hands firmly. "They are always especially bad, according to everyone around here. Please, Tessa, I'll be fine."

Tessa nibbled her lower lip. "You're sure?"

"If we can teach grade school, we can handle

anything nature throws at us. You should know that.''

Tessa chuckled. "I do love teaching. Okay. Don't forget, Drake said if you need to test wheelchairs and such out there, he'd be available to help out.''

"I'm surprised he is willing to get back in one of those things," Leah murmured softly, with feeling.

Tessa's gaze darkened a bit. "He still has his bad days when he has to use one. I imagine he will for a while to come. But I think…well…I think offering to help makes him feel useful. You know, he feels that being in the wheelchair gave him an opportunity to help someone else in need down the road.''

Leah's gaze softened, a warm feeling filling her. "Can you still believe how much God changed Drake's life?''

Tessa's gaze changed from dark to a sweet dreamy smile. "If he hadn't found Him, I wouldn't be with him now. And he's so fresh. I'll tell you, Leah, his freshness is what restored my faith in God. I think I had forgotten just how wonderful and loving our Father is. Seeing it from a new believer's point of view made me realize how lucky I really am and how the past doesn't matter near as much as I thought it would.''

Leah's bright smile faded a bit at the words. In some cases, a past certainly did matter. Her past did matter. Her entire life had changed because of it. She would definitely end up having her entire life changed if it ever became public.

Deciding it best to change the subject, Leah stood. "I am on my way out to the camping area near the Culpepper Ranch. If you need anything else, call."

Tessa stood and hugged her. "Will do."

Tessa had parked on the street, so Leah let her out the front door and locked it behind her. She turned and headed toward the back door and down the steps to her gray compact. Getting in, she prayed that perhaps one day Tessa's words would prove true, that maybe she would find a place somewhere where her past wouldn't matter.

However, she feared, that would only happen with Dan's death.

"She's not here."

Mark paused by the door of his beat-up old Jeep. After slamming it shut, he strolled forward to where Tessa stood. There she was, near her car parked just in front of him, her hand on the door, two books tucked under the other arm. "I had thought to catch her so we could speak of a business arrangement," Mark said, then remembering his manners he asked, "How are you doing, Tessa?"

She smiled. "Fine. I'd be doing a lot better if Leah hadn't just left to go out looking for a site to camp."

Mark leaned on the door of Tessa's car. "She what?"

"She told me she hired you."

"Word travels fast," Mark muttered. "But what was this about a camp?"

Tessa flipped a hand up in a general gesture of airy carelessness. "I was on my way over here but stopped by the station. Your sister, Laura, told me you were going to be working for Leah over the next few weeks. Okay, well she hinted at it," Tessa added tossing her head. "Anyway, when I dropped in to pick up the books Leah had told me I could borrow, I asked her if she'd found someone to take those pictures for her and show her around. Leah's neighbor delighted in telling me the news when I arrived." She cocked her head toward the house next-door where a curtain quickly fell back into place.

Mark shook his head, not used to small towns like this.

"Sure enough," Tessa continued without a pause, "she was glad to have hired you but decided to go ahead and do some legwork herself."

Mark ran a hand down his face. When Tessa got to talking, she really could talk, he thought wryly. "You didn't happen to mention, *chérie,* that the snakes are bad this time of year?"

"I did," Tessa said, grinning.

"Did you tell her there still might be vagrants wandering around after the trouble we had out that way a few months ago?"

"Actually, I didn't, Mark. I figured if snakes didn't scare her, men wouldn't." Eyeing Mark speculatively she added, "Though perhaps that would have been the right excuse to use after all."

"I can't believe she went out there.... She hired me," Mark replied, worried. "Which way did she go?"

"Mrs. Culpepper's," Tessa replied cheerfully.

Mark tilted his head, studying Tessa. "And just why do you tell me this with such a buoyant attitude?" he queried, that Cajun accent slipping back into his speech.

Her grin widened. "Because I am hoping, Mark, that you'll go out there and make sure she's okay."

"Does this entire town worry about that woman?" Mark asked, hands going to his hips, exasperated.

"We sure do," Tessa replied drawing a reluctant grin from Mark. "You didn't think you were the only one, did you?"

"She does tend to bring out that protective instinct, doesn't she?" Mark replied softly.

"She sure does."

"Okay, Tessa. I'll go check on her. After all, it is what I am being paid for," he replied. "To help her out on this project. And when I find her, we'll restate just what we each expect from the other in this job," he added.

Tessa chuckled her deep rich chuckle and replied, "You do that. She's only got about a five or ten-minute start on you. I'm sure you'll find her easily."

"Thanks, Tessa. Tell Drake hi," he replied.

He turned and headed back toward his Jeep wondering just why Leah had headed out on her own without contacting him.

If he had his way, he was about to find out.

After hopping into the Jeep, he quickly left behind the city limits of Hill Creek and headed out toward the west side of town where Mrs. Culpepper lived. At the fourth mile road, as they called them since the roads were laid out so straight, he turned right.

A nice popular camping area located about five miles up was where she'd most likely gone, Mark thought. The Culpeppers owned part of the land. The rest they donated to the county for the people of Hill Creek County. It wasn't to be developed, simply kept there so that there would always be a place for people to camp and wander. Ten thousand acres. When Mrs. Culpepper's husband had passed on she'd said that with no children, she didn't want the land going to the state when she died. She had donated it instead with a provision for a specific use.

She was a town icon, someone that everyone enjoyed and visited. A bit eccentric, but a good old woman. Mark had a notion that she would have made a good mother. He'd gotten to know her through Wil Whitefeather who had been acquainted with the Culpeppers for years.

Driving past Mrs. Culpepper's house, he continued until he reached the small dirt road that led to a parking area. This part consisted of boulders placed in a semicircle on the ground. The area would hold two or three buses and a dozen cars.

He had no trouble spotting Leah's car. Spotting Leah, however, was a different matter.

"Ten minutes. How far could the woman be?" he muttered and killed the engine of his Jeep. Pushing open the door he swung his long legs out and stood, scanning the rocky, hilly area. The summer sun beat down on his head, causing him to lean in, grab his hat and slip it on his head. A wind blew, giving relief to the hot dry air. All was quiet except for the rustling of tree branches as the wind made its music.

Mesquite trees, scrub oaks and sagebrush dotted the vicinity enough to easily block the view of someone within shouting distance. He pulled out the small cylindrical container in his pocket and fished for another toothpick. He continued to scan.

"Leah!"

So he'd shout, he thought, disgruntled. Shouting wasn't his way. But she sure wasn't anywhere in the area. Slipping the toothpick into his mouth he shifted impatiently. The nearby river that crossed the land was an ideal place for people to camp. Perhaps she'd gone out that way.

"Leah!" he called again and started out toward the river.

"Mark?"

He nearly jumped out of his skin when her voice came from behind him. Whirling, he opened his mouth to rail at her and stopped, surprised. "Wil," he said nodding to the old man who stood with her.

"We were scouting the area," Leah said. "I found Mr. Whitefeather out here hunting. He was showing me the bird's nest he'd found."

The aged Native American, his dark weathered skin creasing with a smile replied, "I thought Ms. Thomas might like it for her class."

"I'm sure she would. Thank you for being with her, though."

Leah frowned.

Wil chuckled. "That talk, young one, will get you into trouble."

"That's right," Leah replied. "I'm perfectly capable of taking care of myself." Those words sounded so out of place with that soft-pitched voice.

Mark hadn't planned to say anything in front of Wil, but Leah's words were like waving a red flag in front of a bull. Throwing caution and concern to the wind, he asked, "Oh? Why did you hire me if you could take care of yourself, *chérie?*"

Leah sighed, amazingly still soft-spoken as she replied, "I thought to come out ahead and look over the area. I don't need a bodyguard." Some quick emotion passed across her face, one Mark couldn't identify. It was gone so quickly Mark wasn't sure if he had imagined it. Pausing, he considered her and thought he might have hit a nerve.

"Do you know there are snakes out here?" he prodded gently, thinking to drive home his point. This woman was just too helpless. She didn't need to be out here like this. "And what about riffraff? Be glad it was Wil you ran into and not someone else."

Leah bristled.

"I think, young one," Wil said looking pointedly at Mark, "that you still have not learned patience and trust."

Mark flushed. "Maybe not, Wil, but does she even know how to defend herself?"

"Please don't talk over me like that," Leah demanded firmly.

Guilt touched Mark at her words. "What would you do if a snake blocked your way?"

"Go around it," Leah replied quietly.

With consternation, he realized she was right and because of that he hadn't been able to make his point. So, he tried another track. "You can't do that with people, or some animals. Just ask Drake, *ma petite*," he said referring to the bull that had nearly killed Drake, Tessa's husband.

"Sometimes you just have to put your trust in God," Leah replied.

"Or know how to shoot a rifle, but I see you don't have one with you. Just a backpack. Tell me, Leah, what would have happened if a coyote was out here, possibly with rabies?"

Leah finally flushed. She pushed a strand of blond hair back behind her ear then clasped her hands together. "I am trying to do what has to be done, Mr. Walker. I'm sorry if you don't approve, but then, I'm not as helpless as I look."

Hearing the distress and determination in her voice, he asked, "Is that so?"

"Yes."

Women, he thought and would have rolled his eyes if she hadn't been staring at him.

"Leah, I was nearly killed by a drug gang out in this area. I know you believe what you say, but with your small size, a man could easily overpower you."

Slowly she shook her head.

Disbelieving at Leah's stubborn insistence she could take care of herself out here in the wilds, he glanced at Wil. His face was perfectly blank as he stood there. "You aren't going to comment?"

Wil shrugged. "If she says she can protect herself, I believe her."

Mark sighed, exasperated. "You always were too trusting, Wil. You even took me in when you had no idea who I was."

Wil grinned, his eyes crinkling up, that gray braid of his standing out in stark contrast against his dark skin. "I rely on God to lead me in some things, boy."

There it was again. Wil had said that a lot to him while he'd been out there, telling Mark to let go of his distrust and anger, to trust God more, trust his fellow man.

"Well, let's just see what you'd do if you were

attacked, *chérie,*'' Mark muttered and then, to prove a point, he ran straight at Leah intending to scare her when he grabbed her.

He hadn't expected to go sailing through the air.

With a hard thud he connected with the ground. His head exploded with pain that ricocheted down his body to the tips of his toes.

He wasn't sure how, except Leah held on to his arm, standing above him, still looking completely helpless.

Wil broke into cackles.

''I'm sorry. I hope I didn't hurt you.'' Leah flushed and released Mark's hand. Stepping back she clasped her hands together in a purely nervous gesture.

When Mark recovered from his utter shock he realized he hurt—all over, not just from the initial pain that had flashed in him but from an ache. He wasn't used to someone getting the better of him, especially not a woman—especially not a *helpless*-looking woman. Staring up at her from this angle, he thought she *still* looked utterly helpless. Except that he now lay on the ground feeling every crooked rock that poked him in the back. How had she done that? Wil moved into the picture cutting Mark's view of Leah.

''Come on, young one, get up and take your medicine.'' Wil reached down and with a strong hand helped pull him up until he was on his feet. Every movement reminded him he'd just been lying on the rocky ground.

Mark groaned realizing he was quite sore. "You knew, didn't you Wil?" Mark asked grouchily when he realized Wil still grinned.

"It's in the way she walks," Wil acknowledged. "Always know your opponent," Wil added.

Flushed and definitely put out over what had just happened, he turned toward Leah.

She stood, arms wrapped around her middle, one hand going up to push at her hair before clasping her other hand in front of her. "Are you okay?" She looked so innocent and serene standing there. It was the worry in her eyes that gave away her anxiety. She really was concerned about what she'd just done.

He laughed.

Wil chuckled, too.

Confused, Leah's gaze went back and forth between the two. "I don't understand," she said carefully.

Mark smiled. "It's time for me to eat crow, Leah." Shaking his head he reached down, grabbed up his hat, and slipped it back on his head. "I owe you an apology."

Relief wilted Leah's shoulders and a soft gentle

smile spread across her features. "I really am sorry. It's just some classes I took…"

"Karate?" he speculated.

"Self-defense. The teacher was a black belt in judo."

"Ah," he replied and chuckled again.

"You aren't angry?" Leah asked.

"The way I see it, *chérie,* I had that coming."

"It was sorta reflex. That's exactly how my teacher used to run at me to get me to defend myself. I apologize for not contacting you either, Mr. Walker. I just started thinking that maybe I should come out here on my own…."

He wasn't buying it. The way her eyes slid away from meeting his told him she'd had another agenda. He wasn't upset, though. Just being with her had a strange calming effect on him. But he had to make a point about how dangerous it could be out here, too. He didn't like to think about a woman out here alone where she might get hurt. "Can you shoot a gun, Leah? Can you defend yourself against wild animals? Do you have a cell phone with you?"

"Well, no," she finally admitted.

"No to one or all of them?" Mark gently prodded.

"No to all of them," she confessed.

"Now that is not good, Ms. Thomas," Wil chimed in.

"Please call me Leah, sir," she said.

"And you can call me Wil. This young one over here does." He grinned.

Mark shook his head. "Ignore him. He's so ornery he wouldn't let me call him anything else."

Wil chuckled again.

"I'll leave this to you two. Don't forget Mary is having a potluck dinner for you young folks in a few days."

"Mrs. Culpepper?" Mark asked, puzzled, having not heard of the latest get-together.

He nodded. "She and I are friends," he said to Leah. "I knew her husband for years. He was one of the first settlers out this way."

"I don't want to intrude," Leah protested worriedly.

Mark glanced at her, surprised, then remembered that as quiet and withdrawn as she was, she just might not know all the people around here. "I doubt it'll be an intrusion. Mrs. Culpepper loves company. She hosts these things every so often. They build a big bonfire, and then sit around it and eat and sing and chat."

"Something to think about," Wil added.

"I'll consider it," she replied to both of them.

"Nice meeting you, Leah." Wil waved, obviously having gotten the answer he wanted. He headed over toward the trees and only then did Mark see he had supplies resting over there.

"I like him," Leah whispered softly as Wil headed off back through the trees.

"He's a good old coot," Mark replied.

"What did you mean he saved your life?" Leah asked.

Mark ran a hand over the back of his neck. "It's a long story. I suggest we save it for dinner tonight."

"Dinner?"

"I'm having dinner with Freckles and Julian. I'd like it if you came with me." Mark paused, wondering how in the world he'd just asked her out to dinner like that when he'd only planned to help her in a purely businesslike manner.

"Will they mind? I mean if they don't expect company..."

Mark grinned. "I have a cell phone with me. They'll know you're coming."

As he stared down at the beauty before him he admitted what a jerk he'd been for thinking this woman helpless and fragile. Sometimes things just weren't as they seemed. And he was finding that Leah Thomas certainly wasn't what he'd thought—to his pleasant surprise.

He wondered just what Leah would think if she

knew that he didn't want to leave her side at all. "It's the least I can do after the way I acted, *chérie.*"

Leah finally nodded. Dropping her hands to her sides she said, "Thank you very much...Mark. I'd love to see Freckles and Julian."

And that was that, he thought. He'd just taken a step he had insisted he wouldn't take here in Hill Creek. He'd just asked the teacher out on a date.

Chapter Four

What would he think if she told him she didn't want to be away from him?

Leah couldn't remember a time she'd enjoyed more than exploring the dusty rocky trails with Mark. They'd nearly been late for dinner and only realized it because the sun was dropping low in the sky. That and the fact both of their stomachs were growling.

Quickly they had headed back to their cars and just now had arrived at Freckles and Julian's house.

"It's about time you showed up!" Julian stood near the barn of the ranch where they had just parked, a chain saw in his hand, cut wood littering the ground around him. "I'm clearing out some chores," he continued, and after laying the saw aside, he strolled over to where they stood.

"Hello, Dr. McCade," Leah said formally.

Julian chuckled and shook his head. "Call me Hawk or Julian, but please, there are too many doctors with that last name in this house."

Julian squeezed her fingers warmly and then stuck his hand out to Mark. "I was wondering if you were going to make it to dinner after all."

"I don't live here," Mark replied good-naturedly.

Julian flipped a hand toward the barn and restored bunkhouse. "Close enough that Freckles worries over you. She's certain you aren't getting enough good meals."

"She's probably right. Café food grows old after a while."

"Mark!" Freckles's words drew their attention to the front porch where she pushed through the door, stepping out onto the wooden terrace. Along the long front planks, rockers sat, waiting to be filled for nighttime stargazing. The rails around the wraparound porch reminded Leah of the old-time hitching posts she'd read about in books. Made like many of the ranches out here, they were wooden, stripped of the bark and waterproofed. These posts were newer as Julian and Freckles had been doing renovations on the old ranch house.

"Leah and I made it, *chérie*. Don't you start on me."

Freckles chuckled and came down the path toward the cars, her long curly red hair bouncing as she came. Her stomach protruded with child, and behind her came a herd of kids. Leah heard them all chattering like geese and saw the way they piled out the door, tripping over one another in their haste.

"They're excited to have company," Freckles admitted as she stopped beside Julian and smiled at Leah. Julian rested a hand on his wife's tummy before leaning down to kiss her cheek.

"Hello there, Jimmy," Leah said grinning at the first and youngest child to arrive at their sides. "I suppose it's not every day you have a teacher out here to dinner, is it?"

"Ms. Thomas," Jimmy said excitedly. Grabbing Leah around the legs, he gave her a hug only a ten-year-old could give. "I told you I had sisters. That's Sherri and Cathi. Rebecca and MaMaw are inside. You can meet her but she'll probably go to bed early 'cause she had a big day today."

"I'll have a word with you, Mark," Freckles said and moved toward him.

"Is that so?" Leah smiled down at the young boy and then glanced to the sisters who had come out with Freckles.

"You are going to waste away if you keep missing meals," Freckles said, waving a finger at Mark, taking him to task for being late and not being home enough. The children didn't seem the least bothered that their big sister was shaking her finger at Mark. Julian stood there and smiled bemusedly.

Freckles's sisters were used to this, obviously. Cathi was a small child for her fifteen years, birdlike in her bones and movements. A long dark ponytail hung down her back and light-brown freckles dotted her nose. Were it not for the budding shape, Leah would have guessed her to be younger than her brother. Cathi stood next to her younger brother and rubbed a hand over his hair. He shoved her hand away. Typical interaction for a brother and sister, and both ignored Freckles.

Sherri looked much older than her seventeen years. Her hair was dark auburn, unlike Freckles's own bright-red hair. She was shapely and beautiful and, Leah noticed, seeing where her gaze was, obviously interested in Mark. Still, Sherri didn't interrupt her sister directly though her gaze begged to be noticed as she danced up and grabbed at Mark's sleeve. "I got the results of my SATs today and I'm going to probably have a scholarship. I thought about going to Louisiana. Could you tell me about the universities there?"

Freckles broke off with her diatribe and turned

Cheryl Wolverton   51

toward her sister. "Let's get our company inside
first, Sherri, then maybe later Mark can talk to you
about that."

"You come with me, Ms. Thomas. I want you
to meet MaMaw," Jimmy said, tugging at Leah's
hand.

As if she had never met Phyllis before, Leah
thought grinning at the young boy at her side.
Smiling at Mark she shrugged and grasped the little boy's hand.

"Jimmy, were you going to spend the night with
Tad tonight?" Freckles asked.

"But I want her to meet MaMaw."

"She will in a bit. You should get your things
together and let Sherri drive you there."

"Okay," Jimmy said and raced off toward the
house, forgetting company in the light of spending
the night away from home.

"Can I drive?" Cathi asked excitedly.

"No, you cannot," Julian said, his attention finally diverted from his wife to the girl who looked
so expectantly toward him. "No, you may not.
You're only fifteen and you don't have a driver's
license yet."

"But I have a permit." She smiled brightly as
if that would change Julian's mind. It didn't work,
however.

"And Sherri is only seventeen. She is not old

enough to supervise your driving. No.'' He reached out and ruffled the top of her hair, messing up her ponytail.

Cathi screwed her face up as if she were about to argue.

''Maybe next week I'll take you out driving, Cathi,'' Mark said.

''Really?'' Cathi grinned, her gaze riveting on Mark. When she saw he was serious, her excitement eased and she replied, ''Okay.''

''Go see if the spaghetti is ready, Cathi.'' Freckles shooed her off.

''Do I have to drive Jimmy?'' Sherri asked, casting a glance toward Mark.

Julian frowned though Leah doubted Sherri noticed it as she was so busy trying to look as if she wasn't staring at Mark.

Freckles stepped forward and slipped an arm through Julian's arm drawing his attention. ''Yes, you do,'' she said to her sister. ''And I appreciate all the help you give us out here, Sherri.''

Sherri glanced at her sister then Julian, and with a sigh, she walked off toward the area where the family cars were parked. ''I'll be in the car,'' she muttered.

''It's almost like being in the classroom,'' Leah said half-jokingly when all the children were gone.

"Except they're all different ages?" Julian quipped.

Leah chuckled. "Something like that."

Mark touched Leah on her back between the shoulder blades and motioned toward the door. "Shall we?"

That gentle touch warmed her, reminding her of just why she was out here and whose invitation she had accepted. "If Freckles and Julian are ready," Leah mouthed softly, glancing pointedly at the two who had their heads together talking low.

As if sensing the attention Freckles glanced around and then promptly blushed. "I'm sure dinner's almost done. Let's go eat."

Julian chuckled low, a satisfied smile on his face. "You'll have to forgive Freckles. She has her mind on other things."

"Hawk!" Freckles warned, her cheeks turning a shade darker.

With interest Leah's gaze went from one to the other. The byplay was something that she had long forgotten. It seemed like another lifetime, another person, when she and her husband had done such things. The small touches, wicked grins, secretive smiles. How would her husband have acted if he'd been alive and she hadn't lost her child?

Leah warmed thinking about it, and at the same

time felt a distinct emptiness within her at the hollowness those secret smiles caused.

"It's your announcement. I won't ruin it."

"Announcement?" Mark asked.

"After dinner," Freckles admonished and hurried toward the front door.

"Shall we go?" Julian asked and without waiting for an answer headed off after his wife.

Mark grinned. "I haven't quite figured them out. It seems they are always like this. Involved, that is."

A slight sorrow touching her heart, Leah replied, "It's called love."

Without another word she followed Julian and Freckles, leaving Mark to follow behind.

The screen door creaked as Julian pulled it open, causing Freckles to wrinkle her nose in disgust. "That has got to be oiled, Hawk."

"I will, honey," Julian replied.

Mark rolled his eyes.

Leah grinned.

"Mom, you know Leah. She hired Mark and is joining us for dinner tonight. And this is Rebecca," Freckles said, "as you well know."

Leah, of course, knew Phyllis, otherwise known as MaMaw. Short in size, her mainly dark-brown pageboy hair was gray with age, curled slightly under as it framed her face. She had a tired smile as if she'd seen many hard years, though her eyes shone with an inner peace. Leah knew immediately that inner glow bespoke of her relationship with Jesus Christ. They'd had talks before when Phyllis had stopped by the school for one thing or another.

Then there was Rebecca, Phyllis's middle child. She was a precious child at her age of twelve. Severely handicapped, she was strapped into a wheelchair a lot of the time, but Leah had seen Rebecca make her way around the room, often in her own world as she laughed and played. She was a blessing to all of them, hard to manage occasionally but special in her own way.

"Hi, sweetheart," Leah said squatting down in front of Rebecca now.

Rebecca gurgled and waved a hand, then bounced in her chair.

"I thought Jimmy said she was tired?" Leah asked.

"She's on her last legs," Mark replied. "She always has a spurt of energy as she tries to fight sleep."

Surprised, Leah glanced around at Mark.

"He's right," Phyllis said and stood, leaning down to lift her daughter into her arms. "He's been a big help with Rebecca here. And she just loves him, don't you, sweetie," Phyllis cooed to her daughter, smiling tiredly.

The little girl laughed and wrapped her arms around her mama's neck. As awkward as it was, the child managed to hold on.

Mark grinned. "She's my darlin'," he replied.

"Sorry to run just as you get here, Leah, but I have to put her to bed. Maybe I'll be down later."

"That's fine, Phyllis. We can talk then."

"Say bye-bye," she told her daughter as she started through the house. "Bye-bye," she repeated, talking to her child with all the love a mother had for her baby—even if the baby was twelve years old.

"It was a blessing that she managed to come out here," Mark said.

She turned her gaze to Mark. "Oh?"

He nodded. "You know she was working herself to exhaustion back East. They lived in a tiny apartment and were on constant watch for gangs and trouble. Rebecca has flourished since they've moved here. Even Phyllis is finally looking better, not so exhausted. Julian said Freckles was really worried about her mom."

"I didn't realize you spent much time with them," Leah voiced quietly.

Slipping the toothpick from his mouth he dropped it in a nearby trash can. "I help around the house some. It's the least I can do since Julian has given me some space to live. But don't forget,

Julian, being Zach's brother, is indirectly related to me so I'm around them more than just out here.''

His grin melted Leah's reserves, making her want to stand there and stare at him all night. He looked so mischievous grinning down at her as he leaned there against the doorjamb leading into the dining room. She couldn't help but smile back. "You're brothers-in-law," she agreed.

"Dinner's ready!"

Drawn out of the feelings that had kept the two of them isolated from the others in the area, Leah turned to see Cathi just finishing her chore of setting the dining room table.

"Oh, dear. I didn't even offer to help." Leah clasped her hands together, worry creasing her brow.

Mark reached out and caught her fingers. She jumped, almost pulling back before catching herself. Staring down to where he'd grabbed her hands, his darker ones covering her pale skin, she realized how long it'd been since a man had actually held her hands.

"No reason to be nervous," he said mildly. "That's a bad habit of yours, clasping your hands whenever you're worried."

She swallowed, reminding herself that Mark worked for Mitch—the sheriff. As handsome and attractive as Mark was, she had to get a grip on herself. She couldn't let down her guard so easily. He shouldn't have been able to notice her anxiety. Had she actually fallen so much out of practice since living here in Hill Creek?

Forcing herself to relax, she smiled up at Mark. "I'll remember that."

He cocked his head curiously.

She turned and headed toward the table, where Julian and Freckles were just coming through the swinging door that led to the kitchen. Both had their hands filled with old-fashioned stoneware dishes filled with steaming entrées. Relief touched her as she was finally able to divert her attention elsewhere. However, Leah couldn't help wondering just what Mark might be thinking right now, as quiet as he was behind her.

Mark watched her, wondering if she'd felt anything at all when he'd touched her a moment ago. He hadn't been thinking when he'd reached out. He'd simply acted, and immediately reacted, noting how soft her skin was, how nervous she was around him, how much he'd startled her.

The look in her eyes, the surprise and shock, made him think that people didn't touch her often. She was certainly a mystery, this woman. The more he was around her the more mysterious she became.

And the more attractive. As her eyes had opened

so wide and watched him, he'd seen dark-blue flecks within the light blue of her eyes. He couldn't remember seeing eyes quite that color before.

They were beautiful.

They fit her fragile beauty, as well.

He had to get a grip, and fast. He'd been hired to do a job, not suddenly go into some stage of puppy love. He was too old for this! He didn't want to settle down but liked being a loner. That was why he rarely dated. Dating was for people who wanted to find a mate and marry, not for someone who enjoyed being alone and living their lives as they wanted.

Yet being near Leah made him want to spend more time with her, take her to a movie or out to dinner, somewhere private where he could probe her thoughts, find out her desires and just what and who she was.

Shaking his head, Mark followed Leah to the table, thinking if he didn't keep his gaze off her it was going to be a long night indeed, not to mention a long six weeks helping her.

Chapter Five

Leah bowed her head as Julian blessed the food and company. When the prayer ended Freckles started the dishes around the table. Sherri returned to eat, saying, "A ride came for little brother." She scooted into a chair.

Freckles nodded, smiling.

"So, Julian, Leah here asked me earlier just how Wil had saved my life."

"You were very lucky." Freckles tsked and snagged a piece of bread before passing it on.

"You want me to tell you what happened?" Mark asked Leah.

Leah nodded before dipping the utensils into the spaghetti. "I am curious."

Mark lifted some garlic bread before passing the

plate to Sherri. Taking a sip of the golden-colored tea before him, he thought of how to explain what had happened so long ago.

Julian, at the head of the table, knew some of his story as did Freckles, who sat next to him. Nevertheless they hadn't heard it all. Though Laura had been worried about her little brother, she hadn't confided his past to them. Glancing from Freckles to the woman next to her, Mark wondered if either she or Leah could understand. "I've always been a free spirit," Mark began before scooping up some salad onto his plate. Concentrating on the green leafy vegetable was easier than watching Leah for a reaction. "I suppose that's why I stumbled into photography like I did."

That was partly true. That—and because of his father.

He slipped his napkin onto his lap, then lifted his fork to swirl spaghetti noodles. "I enjoyed my life as a photographer. Feeling as if I'd done it all, I wanted to get away from the Baton Rouge area for a while."

Leah dropped her knife.

The loud resound echoed noisily. Mark glanced up, curious.

"Slippery fingers." She shrugged lamely, then added, "I didn't know you were from Baton Rouge."

Cocking his head, he grinned. "Yeah. New Orleans, Baton Rouge, Lafayette. I've lived in all of them, *chérie.*"

She blinked her eyes showing astonishment. "Oh."

Mark studied her. Interesting that she was curious about his past and hometown. He thought about sharing a bit more with her but then decided he didn't want to make it too obvious to Freckles or Hawk that he was interested in keeping this woman's attention.

"The French and Canadians would cringe in horror over my Cajun accent," he commented. "It doesn't fit in anywhere but in southern Louisiana. Definitely not here, though I think they accept it." He grinned at Sherri who sat next to him. She smiled back.

"I like it," Sherri said.

Mark chuckled at the child. "I'm glad you do." Returning his attention to Leah, he said, "Anyway, I came out here to photograph the Wild West. Out here in West Texas things are much more open, freer to roam. There's more room than back home and different species of animals and birds. I enjoy taking pictures and selling them to magazines and thought this would be a nice change of pace."

"Hill Creek is definitely a change," Freckles added gaily, winking outrageously at Julian who only chuckled and leaned slightly toward her with a private grin.

Mark watched the two bemused lovebirds before pulling his attention back to Leah. He caught her with the fork in her mouth, attempting to slurp up a stray noodle. She flushed when she saw him catch her.

Wiping at her chin she chewed and swallowed. "So, you settled here," she speculated.

"Not exactly. I was here before all that trouble broke out, if you'll remember. Mitch had that deputy sheriff—"

"That almost got my brother killed," Julian added, his gaze darkening.

"And my sister, Laura," Mark added solemnly. "But only because she'd come looking for me." Taking a deep breath, he finally started into the story. "I was out this way taking wildlife pictures when I noticed something strange. Metal reflecting in the sunlight."

"That's not strange," Leah commented. "With all of the windmills and things around...."

"Ah, but remember, I wasn't from around this area and to see something reflecting in an area where I was certain nothing should be made me curious."

He remembered that day well. "I'd seen a scissor-tailed flycatcher, a beautiful bird with a long feathered split tail, perched up on a cactus and had hoped to snap a picture. I'd been there most of the day watching and waiting to snap shots, and just as I lifted my camera, something flashed. It was almost sunset.''

"What was it?" Leah asked.

Brought back by her voice he murmured, "That was my exact question. I mean as hot as it was and dusty out, not many people would wander away from their homes in the middle of the day. As it was nearly sundown, I thought perhaps it was a truck on a back road. You know how you can see for miles. I didn't think any more about it, until I heard a faint sound and saw a reflection again.

"That's when I realized it was an airplane. Very small."

Freckles sighed. "I would expect you'd see a lot of those out here."

"Not exactly," Julian added. "At least not out in the middle of nowhere like that."

"My thoughts," Mark nodded. "I speculated that perhaps they were in trouble. I started over that way until I saw it take off."

"The drug dealers?" Leah asked, curiously.

Mark nodded. "I didn't know it at the time. I thought a house must be out that way. I went home but came back early the next day to capture some more pictures of the sunrise. I traveled farther toward the north and west where I'd seen the flash. I'd been having problems with the Jeep and it'd be nice to know someone in the area in case the car died on me. I thought I might stop by later, introduce myself.''

"That was really brave of you, to go out there, I mean," Sherri chimed in. "You could have been killed."

"I almost was," Mark replied. Tearing off a piece of his bread he chewed on it, giving himself time to adjust to the painful memories. "Unfortunately or fortunately as my father would say, I take after him in the police business. It seems to run in my blood."

Mark tried not to sound too bitter. At least he'd had a father. After swallowing a sip of cool icy tea, he continued. "I got out in the general area where the ranch should have been but didn't see anything. I gave up, thinking I must have gotten my directions messed up or not remembered exactly where I'd seen the plane. I parked in the hills and went back to what I'd come here for, which was pictures. Near sunset I saw it again. A plane, landing. This time I was more suspicious.

I hiked up the hills to find a place where I could see what was going on. They were mostly done with whatever they had been doing by the time I got to a good vantage point."

"Any ideas?" Julian asked, caught up in the retelling of the story, one that Mark really hadn't discussed in detail until tonight.

"Off-loading drugs." Finishing his spaghetti, Mark said, "I slipped down to where I could see and get a closer look while everyone was gone. I got some pictures. That's where I got careless. After finding some stray particles in the back of the plane, I gathered them up in a hankie to take back. I wanted to call my sister for help. Since I was staying in an RV park nearby I didn't know the sheriff. I wasn't sure who could be trusted.

"I started back up the hill, a long hike to go up and back down to get to my car when I heard them returning. I ducked into a nearby cave and dialed my sister on the cell."

"In a cave?" Leah asked, surprised.

"Exactly. Of course, the rocky walls interfered. I had to slip out until I could get a signal—which was really stupid but, with what I'd found and not sure about Mitch, whom I hadn't really met, I wanted to get in touch with Laura. I only had enough time to tell her that I'd found something and was wondering about Zach McCade—"

"Yeah, why were you wondering about him?" Julian asked now, breaking in.

"I knew we were close to McCade property and I was almost certain that Zach owned the land out there. Remember, I'd been all over the place for nearly three weeks by this time. Though I hadn't met many people I did know where most of the people lived, which was why I had wondered about a house out in that area since it should have been so close to Zach's land."

"You thought Zach was...a drug dealer?" Leah gaped at him in total shock.

Mark shrugged. "As I said, I knew few people. I mean, honestly, sometimes you can have lunch with a drug dealer or even a murderer and not have the faintest idea."

Leah paled to a pasty white.

Alarmed Mark leaned forward. "Leah?"

She shook her head, swallowing.

Guilt ate at him for upsetting her. He'd known she was much more sensitive than she let on. He should have been more careful with his words. Where were those manners his grandmother had knocked into his head when he'd been a young child? Probably died with her, he admitted disgustedly. "Don't worry, *chérie,* there are no more dealers out here."

Freckles leaned over touching Leah's pulse and making soothing noises.

"Are you going to throw up?" Sherri asked.

Mark glanced at her, surprised.

"He was brave to stand them off like he did," Sherri added.

Mark shook his head. "I was foolish. Because I called my sister, because I went down there in the first place, those men found me. They thought to make my death look like an accident by pushing me off a cliff." Guiltily, he glanced back at Leah. "I should say no more."

"I'm fine, really," Leah whispered. Her color had come back though it seemed as if a wall had dropped around her.

"I don't want to upset you anymore," he stated.

She actually smiled. "I was being silly. Of course, there are no more drug dealers sitting out there. Do go on. I'd love to hear how Wil enters into this. He seems like such a sweet man."

Mark hesitated noting how Sherri glared at Leah with disgust. He would explain later to the girl that some women hadn't grown up on the street like she had or on a ranch like others in the area. He didn't mind at all that Leah was different, and he should have been more conscious of her sensibilities. But after the way she had flipped him today, he'd let down his guard.

He wouldn't again.

"I was banged up, broken leg, concussion. If the men hadn't heard something and thought that I wouldn't be found, they might have decided to just shoot…ah, finish the job. Instead, thinking the animals would do it for them, they left…''

He winced, then shrugged.

"Please go on," Leah said softly.

Meeting her gaze, he saw that she wasn't upset anymore but really interested in hearing his story. Relaxing, holding her gaze, he continued. "When I woke up I was in a small house, a fire going, lanterns burning. I was covered with a thin sheet and had a cast on my leg."

"Wil?" Leah queried.

"He likes to practice medicine without a license," Julian quipped.

"Hawk, honey—" Freckles warned her husband.

Mark grinned. "That was lucky for me." His gaze left Leah's briefly to acknowledge Hawk and Susan before returning to Leah. "I was banged up from head to toe. I don't remember a time I've felt worse. I had a couple of cracked ribs among other problems. However, when I came to, I found this dark wrinkled man with a long white braid leaning over me."

Leah chuckled. "Wil."

"Yeah," Mark drawled. "I'd been there for three days, in and out of it, muttering. From what I'd said he informed me we should contact Mitch. Since I didn't know who was involved and thought

I'd heard something about a sheriff, I insisted he contact the FBI. Of course, the DEA was contacted. Suffice it to say, strangers showed up one night on his doorstep with someone to check me over and a request to give them all the information I could.''

"They wanted you to help?" Sherri asked excitedly.

"Not exactly. They didn't want me involved, but then, I refused to leave. They figured that as banged up as I was, I couldn't do much damage. Besides, they were hoping if they could get me into town quietly I might recognize someone and point them out.''

"You were in town?" Julian asked, surprised.

Mark nodded. "Wil took it upon himself to be my personal protector. When I was better he told me about my sister—''

"He knew who she was?"

Mark nodded. "He said she looked too much like me and that I'd talked about her in my dreams, warning her away. He felt she was safe not remembering anything since someone had tried to kill her. At least until I was better. He trusted Zach, you see.''

Julian grinned. "My brother is trustworthy.''

"You only say that because he's your brother,'' Mark said, grinning.

"That's right," Julian agreed. "But if you can't trust family, then who is there to trust? Family, I have learned even though I tried to run from it, is the only thing you can count on in time of trouble."

"Except God," Freckles added.

"Except God," Julian confirmed and his gaze went all soft again sinking into the depth of Freckles's gaze. Mark thought he'd never look at a woman like that.

Turning back to Leah, he caught her soft gaze on him and nearly gasped.

Never, not like that but then, to look at her...

"Do you believe in God, Mark?" Leah asked softly.

Mark nodded. "Maybe I drifted a bit over the years, but the near-death experience reminded me of who is in control. And He is about the only one you can depend on."

Leah frowned. "Some families are there for you."

Mark shook his head. "Family is good but only if you can be honest and trustworthy and put them first right after God."

"You sound bitter."

Mark, realizing that was exactly how he sounded, relaxed and said, "Anyway, I came into town several times trying to point out just who I had seen that night. I saw one of the people, though the deputy sheriff wasn't one of them. And I was worried about Laura, how open she was with everyone. Wil, besides taking care of me, made several trips out to the ranch to check up on Laura and let me know if anyone was too near the ranch. When word came from Wil that he'd seen someone skulking around, the agents decided to step up their surveillance. They were supposedly narrowing in. However, I believe without Wil there protecting me, seeing to my mending and keeping an eye on my sister, things would have turned out very differently.''

"Wow," Freckles said.

Mark nodded. "Wow indeed, *chérie*."

"On that note," Freckles interrupted, "I'd like—we'd like to make an announcement."

Mark politely turned his attention to Freckles.

"That's right," Leah said. "Now it's time for your exciting news. Don't keep us in suspense."

Freckles stood and grinned. "Hawk and I would like to announce that we are expecting twins."

"We never do anything halfway it seems," Julian murmured proudly and patted his wife's very rounded stomach.

Leah squealed, delighted, and stood, reaching for Freckles. "Congratulations."

Mark rose to his feet, as well, to shake Julian's hand when, of course, Freckles's timing happened.

Turning green she gasped—and ran to the bathroom.

What an interesting ending to a nice dinner, Mark thought, turning from the table to keep from turning green himself.

"Oh! I'm—I'm—I'm so-o-o—" Freckles groaned from the other room.

Mark met Leah's gaze and together they both burst out laughing at the situation.

"We're practically family," Leah called out toward where Freckles had disappeared. "It's quite all right. Twins," she added more to herself and Mark.

Julian, who had taken off right after his wife, called out, "Meet you in the living room."

"I am never having kids," Sherri announced with disgust and started gathering the dishes.

"You'll never understand the joy until you hold your own child in your arms," Leah said softly.

Mark who had just reached Leah's side paused, hearing that sad note in her voice. He had to wonder if she knew that joy from experience or from yearning for the experience.

One thing was for certain, he shouldn't be wondering about that unless he was far more interested than he should be. Because of that knowledge, he wasn't willing to go that direction with his thoughts. So, ignoring the comment he touched Leah's elbow. "To the living room it is," he called out to Hawk and together he and Leah headed off in that direction while Mark continued to fight that niggling question that had surfaced in his mind.

Did Leah want children?

Chapter Six

Leah sat on a rocker on the front porch, watching Mark as he leaned against the wooden beam that held up the overhead roof. "Freckles gets sick quite a bit?" she murmured softly.

Mark glanced at her. "I think she might have been hiding it." After lifting his feet from the lower beam, he crossed the darkened porch and dropped into another rocker. It squeaked as he adjusted his large frame. Leah leaned back in her own chair, looked up at the starry night and thought how very peaceful it was there.

In town, there was always light and noise. "It's so dark here. You can see so many stars."

"All the way to the horizon," Mark agreed. Lifting a hand, he pointed, "There's Orion's Belt. And over there you can see the Milky Way."

"In all the time I've lived here, I think this is the first time I've sat out in the country and observed the stars."

"Is that part of the reason you want to go out on this trip with the children?" Mark inquired gently.

The sound of crickets echoed along with the occasional swish of grass from the night wind. "You tell me, Mark. What is it that drew you out to take those pictures?"

The porch creaked as Mark started his rocker moving back and forth. "The beauty, maybe. The isolation. Standing out there taking pictures, surrounded by nothing except creation, it reinforces that there is a God."

"I agree," she murmured. "How can a person doubt when they look at the beauty written in nature?"

With her toe, she set her own chair moving gently back and forth, back and forth. "I heard that you were out there the night Laura almost got shot," she said now, continuing with the story from inside.

Leah heard Mark's soft breath, heard as he shifted in his chair and finally how the chair ceased its movement.

"Yeah," he finally admitted, his deep voice curling around her with its tone. "I guess, being there, seeing my big sister almost die...it made me think, Leah.''

Leah nodded, though she knew Mark couldn't see her. He was only a shadow himself.

"When Mitch offered her a job and Laura asked me to stay on, I thought I might just do it.''

"Do you like your job, Mark?''

"I suppose,'' he said after only a short time. "I'm not sure what I want to do.''

Leah hesitated before saying, "For many, being a police officer is in the blood. Either you want to do it and will do it, or you can walk away. I've never really seen anyone in between.''

Mark didn't comment on her statement. Instead, he asked, "Do you like your job, Leah?''

Leah smiled into the darkness. "Working with five-year-olds all day? Yeah, I do. They're a great bunch of kids, so trusting, so accepting, never asking too many questions that shouldn't be asked but honestly curious about everything.''

"Never asking questions?'' Mark sounded as if he didn't believe her.

She chuckled. "Not the type of questions you don't want to be asked. Personal questions about—'' Leah realized what she was thinking and reined in her words. "Well, let's just say they ask everything from how old I am to if I was alive during the Civil War. I can handle those.''

Mark's chuckle answered her. "So, were you?"

"Was I what?" Leah asked.

"Alive during the Civil War?"

Leah gasped, her rocker squeaking abruptly. "You're awful!"

Mark's chuckles grew. "I was kidding. Honest."

"Kidding about what?" Freckles questioned, pushing through the screen door with Hawk as they came out onto the porch.

"He asked if I was alive during the Civil War," Leah replied, her voice filling the night air with her incredulity.

"Mark!" Freckles moved past Leah, pulled Mark's hat off his head and smacked him with it.

"Whoa, there!" Julian said and jumped after his errant wife.

Leah broke into gales of laughter.

Mark yelped and ducked, only spurring Leah's laughter on. "Thank you, Freckles. It feels nice to be avenged," Leah said.

"That's my wife, the avenger," Julian muttered and eased her on down the porch to a swing near the end.

"I just love it when you call me that," Freckles replied cheekily before seating herself on the swing.

Leah's laughter faded as Mark straightened his

hat and started his rocker going again. "Mrs. Culpepper is having another get-together soon out at her house. Wil told me earlier today," he informed Freckles and Hawk.

"Yeah. We'll be there. You attending?"

"Probably. Wil asked Leah to be there, too."

"Oh, you should come," Susan Freckles McCade urged. "They're such fun. They're so old-fashioned."

Leah smiled. "Watch that word, *old*," she murmured, to which they all chuckled.

"So how is the project coming along, Leah?" Julian asked as they all subsided into quiet enjoyment of the night.

"I've got almost everything done. We should be ready on time. Are you going to be able to be the doctors for our trip?"

"You're going to have doctors? Isn't that a bit pessimistic?" Mark interrupted.

"Actually," Susan said, purely professional now, "I think it's very wise of her, considering a few of the children have medical problems."

"I concur," Julian added. "It's better, since this is the first year that Leah is doing that, to be safe than to risk something happening."

"Like not having a cell phone around," Mark muttered for Leah's ears only.

"Cell phone?" Freckles asked, overhearing.

"We'll have a cell phone," Leah replied. "Mark is worried because I was out in the wild today without any backup."

"That's not good, Leah," Julian stated.

"I know. I've heard it from others," she muttered.

"And she can take care of herself," Mark said, surprising Leah. "But she has graciously agreed to allow me to give her rifle lessons," he added.

"Good idea," Julian replied and Leah could hear his swing squeak as he set it into motion. From here it looked as if Freckles had leaned over and had her head resting on Julian's shoulder.

A pang touched her as she realized how lonely she was and how much she longed for such touches.

As if reading her mind, Mark reached out and touched her hand. She paused feeling the warmth, enjoying it, until she realized he was only getting her attention. "And you've agreed to start next Tuesday, right *chérie?*"

Leah lifted her gaze to Mark's own darkened one. She wished she could see what emotions were in his eyes right now as he touched her hand.

Acutely aware of the loss as his hand moved away, she replied, "Yes. Tuesday sounds fine."

"Great!" Freckles said. "So, anyone for Bible Trivia?"

Leah wanted to but shook her head. "I should really be going. Can I take you up on that offer later?"

"Aw..." Freckles protested. "I suppose so, if you promise to carry through."

Leah smiled softly into the darkness. Leave it to Freckles to make anyone feel welcomed. "I promise," she vowed.

Mark stood. "I'll walk you to your car."

Leah stood as well. "Thank you for dinner. I'll keep you updated on the progress of the outing Julian, Susan." She nodded in their direction.

"Come back soon," Freckles said. "We don't see you enough in town and it was a pleasure having you out here."

"Thank you. Good night."

Both Julian and Freckles murmured their goodbyes as Leah headed down the porch. She was intensely aware of Mark as he followed behind her. Very obvious was his presence. The darkness made it so much more intimate.

When she got to her car she turned. "Thank you, Mark, for inviting me...."

She trailed off when Mark reached up and cupped her cheek. "Your skin shines out here in the light," he whispered.

She took a trembling breath. "I—Mark..."

Brushing her hair back he dropped his hand.

"Don't worry, *chérie*. I meant nothing by it. I wanted to thank you for coming tonight. I had never thought to enjoy a night like I did tonight. But your simple company enhanced a mundane experience, making it extraordinary."

Leah chuckled albeit a bit weakly. "You and your words."

"I meant it. Don't forget, Tuesday, *chérie*. And if you need anything before then, please call me. I'd hate to have to start camping out on your doorstep to make sure you get your money's worth out of me."

The image of that caused Leah to flush hot then cold. "I promise I'll call," she hastily agreed.

Mark nodded. "Good." He leaned forward and pulled open her door. "Be careful driving home. Do you want me to follow you?"

Leah, who had just gotten her rocketing emotions under control from the vivid image, felt them go right back out of control. This time with irritation. "I thought we agreed I wasn't helpless?"

She could see his smile from the reflection of the interior light of her car. "You have no cell phone. Until you have one, you shouldn't be out in the country at night, away from everyone—alone."

"I know what away from everyone means," she replied.

He chuckled. "You aren't as shy and withdrawn as you lead most to believe. I like that. I think we'll get along fine, Ms. Thomas. Indeed I do."

"I'm Leah. And if you don't stop treating me like a helpless hen, we won't."

Mark chuckled. "Very well. You are proving you are more than capable of taking care of yourself but…"

Slipping his cell phone out of his pocket, he pressed it into her hand. "You will take this with you."

"But—"

"No buts. Drop it at the sheriff's office tomorrow. I'll get it when I go into town. I want to know you're safe."

And with that, her irritation fled to a warm melting feeling. How very considerate. "Thank you," she said, overwhelmed with how much that small gesture meant to her.

"You should be taken care of, Leah, and not have to depend only on yourself. Let us in—the community. We all want to be your friends."

He squeezed her hand emphasizing his words. "As do I."

"I—I can't, not completely," she whispered.

"One day," he countered firmly, yet with understanding. "One day."

He tightened his grip slightly again, then released her hands. "Travel safely, *chérie.*"

"Thank you." Leah quickly slipped into her car and pulled the door shut. Starting it up she backed away and then swung it around. As she left the drive, she saw Mark Walker still standing where he'd left her, watching as she drove off. "Dear Father, what am I going to do?"

Chapter Seven

"Are you sure this is necessary?" Leah asked, uneasily getting out of her car and walking to where Mark stood. She'd almost been late, rushing about at the last minute to get everything taken care of before spending her day out here with Mark. She had to admit, part of her nervousness of facing this man again had added to her putting off driving out here.

She came to a stop next to Mark's Jeep, noting that Mark waited for her out in the open field just south of town where they'd agreed to meet. The overcast cloudy sky did not appeal to Leah as an ideal situation for learning to shoot.

Especially with Mark. He looked handsome today in his dark blue jeans and cowboy boots, the white shirt clinging to him as he opened the rifle to check the ammunition.

"Just a thunderstorm in a couple of hours or so, Leah," he murmured as she approached, his gaze not meeting hers, instead intent on his actions. "No tornadoes," he said matter-of-factly.

Leah thought back to when she'd been caught in a tornado, her fear resurfacing momentarily. "The only problem with this part of the country," she murmured, "is the unpredictability of tornadoes."

When Mark snapped shut the rifle, she jumped. "I could hire someone to come along perhaps, to carry a gun while we're out in the wild," she offered, her gaze touching the shiny metal barrel of the weapon he held.

Mark finally aimed the gun safely away and smiled his devastating smile. "Everyone out here should know how to shoot a rifle, *chérie*. It's one of the first things Wil taught me when I moved here. It'll do you good. It's for your own good. Besides, anyone who can handle their judo the way you can shouldn't be scared of a gun."

Moving up next to her, he asked politely, "How was your day today?"

"Hectic. Tessa came back for a different book for Drake because he finished the other one he'd borrowed, and my neighbor needed me to take her to the store because her car is broken-down and you know how she is.'' Leah smiled, still affected by his proximity. She had wondered if the other night had just been an aberration from her normal ability to stay detached from society. Realizing she had paused, she continued, ''Mrs. Mulching insists I not drive over ten miles an hour, bless her heart. I also had to stop by the church. Joey's dad is in the hospital and the women are making food for the family until he can get out. Then I had to go home and change before coming out here. How about you?''

He grinned. ''My day has been much calmer. My alarm went off at five. I drove out southeast of here to shoot the landscape pictures. Later I stopped by Zach's to pick up a metal barrel and then went by the office to let my sister know where I'd be in case, for some reason I can't fathom, she might need to know.''

Leah laughed at his long-suffering sigh in his voice when he said the last.

''I'm sure she's not interested in what you're doing out here.''

Mark rolled his eyes. ''Actually she acted very disappointed. You see, I wouldn't be in this evening in time to meet Henrietta, the assistant secretary at the library whom she just happened to invite over for dinner.''

Leah chuckled. "Setting you up?"

Mark sighed. "Constantly. Meddling big sisters never stop."

"I wouldn't know," she said lightly, still laughing.

"So, *chérie,* are you ready for your lesson?"

Leah sobered and studied the rifle he held in his hand. "I guess so," she murmured.

Mark came over and held out the gun to her. "There are several things to remember. As I mentioned the other night after dinner, guns are good to have around but they're dangerous. Always treat a gun with respect."

"You don't have to worry about me on that account," she said quietly.

"Now let's get to know our weapon," he said and then proceeded to show her each piece of the rifle. Thirty minutes later, after answering questions Leah had, he set about showing her how to shoot it. Positioning it against her shoulder, he helped her adjust to the feel of the heavy metal in her hands, held the way she was supposed to hold it. It was long, the front of the barrel, feeling as if it wanted to point down instead of toward the target a few yards away. Such an unnatural feeling, she thought, working to hold the barrel level.

Mark moved around and, standing behind her, he took her shoulders. "Turn like this," he added, twisting her into position. "This is the posture you stand in when you're shooting. You're supporting the rifle, and your body won't take as much kick and be likely to get knocked off balance," he said. "Does it feel easier to hold like this?"

"Yes," she said, thinking it did just slightly. "What do we shoot at?"

"The rusted barrel out there in the field. The one I picked up from Zach," he added, referring to an earlier conversation. "Now that you have your body in position, let's talk about your head. You should tilt your head just so," he added and reached up to help her adjust. "This way you are looking down the sites. See what I'm talking about there?" he asked and touched the different areas on the rifle.

Leah murmured a positive grunt. She didn't like him standing right behind her while she tried to line up her shot. Nor did she like the way he touched her. It had been so long since she'd had companionship with a male—a close relationship. She missed it, horribly. She hadn't realized it until his touches reminded her.

She hadn't really been attracted to anyone, until Mark had come to town. She'd noticed him immediately. Anyone with the sheriff she would, of course, want to know about. She had found herself both wary and drawn to Mark, though she only just admitted that to herself. When she'd had dinner with him the other night at Susan and Julian's house she'd realized that she couldn't deny her interest any more.

She had really enjoyed herself, more than she had in years.

She'd gone home and been unable to stop thinking about how nice it'd been to have someone to sit and talk with, and to trade chuckles with.

Leah was happy to sit and talk freely, not guarding her words and actions as she should, not putting up a shield but yearning to sit and talk.

She'd prayed about it, asking God to forgive her for the things in the past and to please help her control the feelings of attraction and interest. These feelings were making her face too many things she had buried. She didn't want to confront those memories, those consequences, but dinner had opened so many old wounds, so many old yearnings. She'd felt things she hadn't felt since her husband's death, things she had thought never to feel again. Things that made her vulnerable had surfaced.

"Now *chérie,* squeeze the trigger," Mark murmured, bringing her back to the present.

The warmth of his breath against her neck made her pull the trigger. But she wasn't ready for it and stumbled back against Mark.

"You're too tense," he replied, catching her briefly against his wide chest. That certainly felt nice, she thought with sad longing. Too nice.

When he righted her and slipped the rifle from her hands, she breathed a silent prayer of thanks and a hope that maybe it might happen again. "I'm not that tense," she replied, working to push memories of the past aside. Still, she couldn't completely forget. "It's just that guns kill people."

Mark must have heard something in her voice. She had quickly learned how very astute he was at doing that. His smile faded as he opened the gun and laid it aside. He hooked Leah's elbow and led her to a nearby boulder where they sat.

"What are you doing?" she asked, embarrassed and just a bit uneasy by his actions.

"I think we should talk."

"We're here for a shooting lesson, Mark. I didn't mean to imply that I wouldn't try. I simply stated I saw no reason for it when I could hire someone and…"

Mark nodded, tipping his hat back on his head before tossing his toothpick aside. She trailed off realizing there was no reason to argue. It was nerves.

He slid closer to her and he leaned back, crossing his ankles and staring up at the cloudy sky.

"Have you ever been around guns, Leah?"

The way he said her name, so soft and matter-of-fact, made Leah think of idle conversation. Days of flowers and church picnics and passing the time before going home in the evening to relax with a pleasant smile at the friendships made and fellowship had.

The subject, however, grounded her to reality, a reality she had hoped to forget. "Yes," she finally admitted, trying to figure out just how much to reveal.

Surprised, Mark turned toward her. "Really?"

Leah stared back. "Did you expect me to say no?"

Mark grinned. "Actually, I did. Tell me, *chérie,* where did you become familiar with guns?"

Leah hesitated.

Mark quirked an eyebrow studying her. "I think it is some time in the past you do not want to discuss, yes?"

Leah chuckled, momentarily diverted from the heavy feeling of her past to ask, "How do you do turn your accent on and off like that?"

"Perhaps, *chérie,* it's a secret of mine like you have for you."

She frowned.

"Okay, okay. I won't push. When I am worried or stressed my accent tends to thicken, until some-

one points it out.'' He grinned, pulled out a toothpick and popped it in his mouth. ''Now, your turn.
Tell me something about yourself which no one
else knows.''

''Why?'' she asked curiously.

He grinned. ''Telling me a secret will hopefully
ease some of your anxiety.''

Leah simply stared at him before bursting into
laughter. ''That's—that's— Has any woman ever
fallen for that line before?''

Mark chuckled. ''We'll find out in a moment.''

Sitting there as he did, leaning back against the
boulder, looking up at her with his quirky expression, she gave in.

''I am an only child.''

Mark gave her a wide-eyed stare before saying,
''Mais non!'' Hitting his forehead with his hand
he grinned. ''I would not have known, *chérie.*''

She found herself smiling at him. ''How could
you tell?''

''I am a youngest child. My best friend is an
only child. You don't have a dictatorial attitude
like a big sister and you do not act spoiled as many
youngest children are—''

''Like you?'' she asked.

He grinned. ''Like me.'' Something dark passed
quickly in his eyes before he added, ''You act
more responsible than others I know so I would

guess you were raised by older parents as an only child.''

Amazed, Leah nodded. "You're right."

"And from your accent I'd put you from the South, Mississippi or Louisiana most likely."

Leah paled.

"However, where you are from doesn't matter," Mark said as if he knew revealing her birthplace bothered her. "I am sure anyone knows what you told me. So, tell me something else."

"This is silly," Leah said, starting to clasp her hands before she remembered Mark pointing out her nervous action the other night. Balling her hands into fists, she put them by her thighs instead. "I'm wasting your time and mine."

"Not at all," Mark said. "Actually, there is method to my actions, *chérie*. You're too tense to fire a rifle right now so I wanted to talk. I also had ulterior motives."

Her heart thudded at those words.

She wasn't ready for Mark's hand to ease up and touch her own hand. Glancing down at his dark hand she shivered. "What are those motives?"

"Since Freckles and Julian's spaghetti dinner the other night I've been thinking, Leah."

She was glad she wasn't the only one, she thought disgruntled, remembering how she'd not been able to sleep a night through since then. "About what?" she prodded.

Mark turned Leah's palm face up and traced her fingers, causing Leah's jaw to drop.

His gaze lifted to hers. "I don't think I am the only one who felt an attraction between the two of us, *chérie,* and—"

Leah quickly pulled her hand away, clasping both hands together nervously. So much for not letting him see her sweat, she thought.

"Please hear me out," he said. The teasing gone from his voice, he sat up. Lifting himself until he sat on the boulder next to her, he continued, "I had the feeling you were as disconcerted as I by the fact. Believe me, I'm not interested at all in a permanent relationship."

"Good. Neither am I," Leah replied quickly, dizzy with where the conversation had turned.

"However, it would be nice to get my sister off my back if I had someone to date occasionally, perhaps as friends, someone I could be comfortable with."

Leah heard the words and simply blinked. "Excuse me?"

Mark must have realized how his words sounded because he held up a hand. "I didn't mean to say you weren't dateable—"

"You're digging yourself in deeper," Leah replied wryly, crossing her arms and staring at the man before her. She enjoyed his sudden discomfiture. How long had it been since she'd teased a man, flirted with him, or joked? Especially a man who could take it, like Mark?

Mark ran a hand down his face. "I thought, perhaps, I know Freckles has been trying to find a husband for you as much as Laura has been looking for someone for me. I found I like the idea of helping you, *chérie,* set up this picture shoot and outing. I thought a few evenings together as friends might get my sister off my back."

Leah started to respond when she saw something in his eyes, something she well remembered in her father's eyes years ago after her mother had died. Something she'd felt many times throughout her years of traveling after the loss of her husband and child. Loneliness.

Mark was lonely and seeking out companionship. Not looking to settle down or marry but to have a close friend, someone to share with; he was asking her to fill that position.

"I—" Leah started feeling her own need to respond out of her depths of loneliness.

"I apologize, Leah." Mark glanced away when she hesitated. "I hadn't meant to bring up the subject like this, and not today, but since the other night I thought—"

"Yes."

Mark glanced back at her. "What?"

"I— Well, yes. It might be nice. I mean, I have the entire town worrying after me, though they think I don't notice. Maybe going out occasionally will convince them I'm not made of blown glass."

She had to be crazy. What had she just agreed to? And with whom? The man who had the sheriff's ear? But she wanted to, she realized. She had grieved a long time for her husband, her grief mixed with anger and finally acceptance. Suddenly the future, living in her own world, never actually interacting with anyone because of her fears, seemed to stretch out indefinitely. She saw herself as Mrs. Culpepper, alone, in a house, no children...hiding away the rest of her life.

Mark studied her. "You are sure this won't offend you?" Taking her hand he continued, "I know you hired me for a job. And I suppose I am crazy to even ask it of you, but it just seemed right."

"Funny," Leah said softly, her eyes crinkling with amusement as she realized that with this man who had been so up-front, she could actually change that picture she had of herself and at least start living again. Her past was that, her past. He would never find out about it, and what were the chances of anyone from her past finding her here? "I didn't think of you as the impulsive type."

Mark chuckled. "Now you are teasing," he added just as quietly. "Let me say something which might ease you on that area, *chérie*. I am impulsive, yes. It is because I did not like what I left and sought something more."

How long had it been since anyone had been honest with her? How long had it been since anyone treated her like she might be able to help? Not like she needed to be cared for, but as if she could actually care for them?

"Have you found what you're looking for yet?" she asked quietly, wrapping her own hand around his larger one.

He shook his head. "I'm not sure, Leah. Being out here, taking pictures, seemed like the ideal job for a while. I enjoy it but..."

"Have you prayed about it?" Leah asked.

"Now you're sounding like my sister." Shaking his head, he admitted ruefully, "No, I haven't."

"Why?"

Mark started to reply then shrugged. "It's not important. What is important is the fact that I think we can help each other. And it'd be nice to have a friend in town other than Mitch's family and Freckles's family."

Leah chuckled. "Sherri has a crush on you, you know."

Mark blinked. "No. I didn't know."

Leah nodded. "It's not uncommon for young girls her age. Be careful with her."

"I've watched their family fondly," Mark confided now. "They're so close, so...open with each other."

"Your family wasn't?" she asked.

"My dad wasn't around much," he replied. "And now you're relaxed. So, what do you say we go back to practicing? This time we'll take it slower and I won't rush you."

Leah definitely felt the barricade go up over the conversation of his family. Evidently he hadn't had a good childhood. Was that the reason he had left home?

She definitely wasn't going to go where he didn't want her to go. And he'd been polite enough to back off any time she'd gotten uncomfortable, too.

"Very well. Though, I have to say, Mark, this has been the strangest few minutes I think I've experienced in the last few years."

Mark chuckled. "It's all part of my plan. Remember? To make you relax and enjoy."

Leah shook her head. "Let's just get to shooting

and maybe we can meet over dinner Wednesday after church to discuss this.''

Mark's eyes twinkled. ''Are you asking me out on a date, Miss Leah?''

She blushed.

He laughed. ''I like the bolder you. And I accept. Wednesday it is. Now back to work.''

He stood and offered Leah his hand. She took it, wondering what she had gotten herself into with this man, and not sure if she ever wanted out.

Chapter Eight

With her head down against the gusty wind, Leah hurried into the diner. Dressed in a pale-blue pullover dress, she'd caught her blond hair back, pinning it to the back of her head. She pulled back strands that had fallen out around her face.

Heading to a back table, she smiled and waved at the different people in the diner. She knew them all, though she wasn't really close to any. She noted Suzi's daughter playing near the jukebox and waved when the little girl called out to her.

Seating herself, she smiled as Suzi walked up with a menu. "I'm expecting someone. Can you leave two menus?" she asked.

"Sure." Suzi set down a second menu and smiled. "Want me to bring you some tea, *señorita?*"

"Please. Thank you. Your daughter is really growing," Leah added softly thinking how Suzi glowed since her marriage to Mitch.

"*Sí.* I can't wait for her to start school next year. She's already excited about her new grade at school."

"She did excellent in my class. I imagine after school starts they'll want to put her in some accelerated classes."

Suzi beamed. "I'm proud of her. So is Mitch."

Leah smoothed her dress before folding her hands on the table. "You have every right to be."

"I'll be right back with your tea."

Suzi turned to leave and passed Mark who was strolling down the narrow aisle. Mark caught her and ordered some tea for himself before continuing on to the table. If she was surprised to see Mark seat himself next to her, Suzi didn't show it.

Tossing his hat next to him, he said, "I went by your house. You weren't home."

Dismayed, she asked, "Was I supposed to meet you there?"

Mark chuckled that easygoing chuckle of his. He looked good in the white shirt and dark blue jeans. "Relax, Leah. I didn't know where we should meet so I stopped by there. When you weren't home I came on over here. I just didn't want you to think I'd stood you up."

Leah smiled, relaxing. "I didn't. Since I live in town it was easier to walk. It's only three blocks."

"Do you like living in town?"

Leah smiled. "Actually, I do. Small-town life is wonderful. Everything is within walking distance and with so few people there are never too many cars out."

"Coming from a large town I can say living out in the country is certainly different, though the travel time to get anywhere is about the same."

Leah nodded. "I like not having to drive a car often." She opened her menu.

Mark followed suit.

Suzi arrived with their tea. "So, are you ready to order?"

Leah shifted the menu closing it. "I'll have your grilled chicken salad and soup of the day."

"Steak," Mark murmured.

Suzi wrote the order down and hurried off.

"I'm surprised she still works. This is a hard job. Since she and Mitch married I had thought she'd quit."

Mark shook his head. "She's helping out. Mitch said she plans to cut way back when school is in, but agreed to assist for the next few weeks here. I think she is waiting to hear on that new company out west, just fifteen miles away. She's applied for a secretarial pool or some such. It's part-time status. She really doesn't want to work, but at the same time wants to bring in some income.''

"I guess since she's worked all her life...."

Mark nodded. "If you had the choice, *chérie*, would you work?"

Leah paused. "I'm not sure. I love spending time with children, teaching them, exploring different things but..."

"But?"

"How about you? Would you work if you had to?" she asked grinning at him.

"I am working. Doing what I like. I set my own hours...."

"At the sheriff's office?"

Mark shook his head. He hesitated and she saw a flash of something—she wasn't sure if it was disappointment or a simple loss of something before he said, "I'm pretty sure I won't go back to that job. Mitch gave me six weeks off, but I've thought about it and am almost certain when my time is up I'll put in a resignation."

Surprised, Leah stared. "Why?" She would have sworn just the opposite would be true.

"I appreciate my sister getting me the job, but I have other ideas of what I'd like to do." His gaze touched the features of her face.

Leah felt herself warm, wondering if she'd just read something into his look that he hadn't meant.

Or had he meant he would rather be with her? She wasn't even sure she wanted to admit it to herself. Had he intimated he was interested in pursuing a relationship with her rather than working as a police officer?

"You mean as a photographer?"

Another hesitation and then he nodded. "Yes. That and...other things." With a shrug he added casually, "My father had no time as we grew up. He was always gone. I'm not sure that would be what I wanted if I decided to pursue relationships as I see fit."

Leah blinked, certain now that his gaze earlier had meant what she'd thought. "I...see."

"You know how it is, with someone in the force, *chérie*," Mark said now his gaze not meeting hers as it went to the window, staring out at the street.

Leah thought about her husband and had to admit she did know what it was like with someone on the force. She also had to wonder if Mark was making the right decision. It alleviated some anxiety to think he might not be going back into the sheriff's office where he might find...

"They are often gone for long periods of time, away from home, leaving the family to raise itself. I'm sure you've seen Mitch do that, though he has started delegating what he can since he's married.

Still, he is gone a lot, much more than I think would be good for a family.'' Mark shrugged. ''I don't want that for my life. I want something else.''

Leah nodded and again said, ''I see.''

''See what?'' a voice behind them said.

Leah jumped at the sound of Mitch's voice, her gaze jerking up to the man who had somehow made it all the way down the row without her noticing.

''Daddy!'' Suzi's daughter came running and launched herself into his arms.

''Hi there, pumpkin,'' he said squeezing her tight.

Leah thought it was wonderful the way the young child called her stepfather daddy. She smiled fondly and realized her child would have been close to the same age as Kristina if she'd lived.

She sighed, melancholy touching her. She was lonely and envied the way Mitch held the child so closely.

''Go tell Mommy I'm here and ready when she is.''

''Okay!'' She jumped down and scampered off.

''Have a seat,'' Mark said, his grin turning sardonic as Mitch slid in next to him. Leah glanced from one to the other wondering why Mark looked as he did toward Mitch.

"We were talking about how you spend way too much time at work and not enough time at home."

Mitch scowled. "Not that again. Suzi and I are comfortable with the hours I work. I work forty and then only more if there is some emergency."

Mark smiled the indolent smile of his. "It is still too much, my friend." Shrugging, he added, "I saw it tear families apart."

Mitch shook his head. "It's how you set your priorities. I hope you pray about this before you quit on me."

Leah nibbled her lip, uneasy at being privy to such a conversation. Mitch and Mark both must have realized the inappropriateness of it for Mitch turned and asked, "Tell me, Leah, did you enjoy teaching back in Philadelphia?"

Leah nodded, her hands clasped below the table. "I've always enjoyed teaching. It's nice. I love children. They're wonderful to work with."

Mark, either sensing her discomfiture or just deciding to fill Mitch in, shifted the subject. "Things are going well on the planning. Leah is learning to shoot a rifle and we have the general area narrowed down to where she wants to take the children. I have enjoyed going out and doing this for Laura and Leah."

"Good to hear," Mitch replied. Suzi chose that moment to walk up.

"Meli will be bringing your food. I'm off."

Mitch glanced up at her and his gaze softened the lines of his face, easing into a genuine smile. Reaching up, he snagged her hand before standing. "We'll talk to you later," Mitch said nodding to Mark. "Nice chatting with you, Leah."

Slipping his arm around Suzi he started down the aisle. Suzi's daughter was outside, balancing on the curb while she waited.

"They look so happy together," Leah murmured softly.

"They are," Mark replied, nodding to Meli who deposited their food before them.

He couldn't help but stare at the soft, gentle expression in Leah's eyes as she watched the two walk away. He would catalogue the look as one of longing if he had to put a tag on it.

It seemed the teacher was interested in more than she let on. The other day when he'd confessed his desire to hang out with her he'd been a coward. What he should have said was he found her fascinating and was interested in getting to know her better. But as jumpy as Leah was he just hadn't been able to admit that to her then.

Sitting here with her now, he noted an emotion in her, the same emotion he'd felt though he'd denied it when he'd been talking with her. He saw loneliness and longing reflected in that gaze of hers—something that mirrored his own heart.

He'd run from home, missing out on what he saw. The only one who had what he'd searched for, he'd found, was his Heavenly Father. And while that had been enough when his earthly father hadn't been there for him, he found he wanted something else now, something his father could not have ever filled. He wanted companionship with a woman.

He had vowed at one time that he'd never be interested in that, simply because he'd seen what his father had been like with his family. But watching this woman, longing for her, seeing something special in her that was easily loveable, he found that this was more important to him than staying away.

He wanted to get closer to her.

One way to do it was to simply ignore his desire to be a police officer. He had a built-in excuse. He didn't want to do it simply because his father had wanted it for him. But the excuses—they could really quell the desire in him. With Leah's attitude toward the police and his experience with a father who was a cop, he knew it had to be either/or—it couldn't be both.

Shaking his head, he smiled when Leah's attention turned back to him. It was time he found a wife and settled down. "I really like this area out here," Mark confided now as he started to work on his steak. "I've been thinking of buying a small piece of land in town, moving here, but I'm not sure if I'd like living this close."

"Really?"

He shrugged. "As I said, I'm not sure. I do think I plan to stay in this area, however. I've found the people friendly."

Leah swallowed a bite of her salad and said softly, "And Freckles and Julian have adopted you into their family."

Mark nodded. "I'm still a bit uneasy and unsure how to act with that. They are certainly special," he confided.

He took another bite of his steak before continuing. "Tell me, Leah. Would you continue to teach if you had an option?"

Furrowing her brow, she finally admitted, "I don't know. There are other things I've thought about doing. I enjoy teaching but I think I'd rather teach children with special needs."

It was Mark's turn to be surprised. "Really?"

She nodded. "I have thought before of possibly being a special education teacher or even going into occupational therapy."

"I bet Tessa or Susan could help you with that

area," Mark commented, fascinated by what Leah had just revealed.

"How did you get into photography? Was that your original job?"

Mark shook his head. "I've done several different things. However, I've taken pictures since high school. It drove my father crazy, probably why I kept it up." Mark smiled though the thought didn't give him much happiness. He and his father had wasted so many years fighting. He wished he could go back and change it but... "Only two years ago did I really start doing it full-time. I was fed up with big-city life and floating from job to job. I'd worked in a police station, fire station, newspaper office..."

Sighing, he said, "I wanted something else so I left, coming out here to take pictures and try to decide which direction my life was going to take."

"And what did you find?" Leah asked conversationally. He didn't think she had any idea just how hard that question was to answer.

"I found a church that taught me to seek God first." He admitted he still hadn't thought about this one subject though. "I found a family that has taken me in as their own." Where his father hadn't been there, God had replaced him with this new wonderful family and even brought his sister out here, making her a part of it. "I've found I like the peace and quiet of the small town."

It was away from all of the old memories and giving him time to heal.

Leah paused with her salad. "But you still don't know what you want to do permanently?"

He sighed. "Perhaps I am doing it now," he said. "Perhaps this."

But he knew, as he said it, there was more, much more he should be doing, like letting go completely of his past and forgiving his father. Until he did that, he wouldn't be free and couldn't make a tough decision on his future.

Leah lay her fork and knife down. "I know this is hard to say, Mark, but perhaps, if you let go of past hurts, then you might be able to see more clearly."

Mark stiffened, his gaze riveting to her. "What makes you say that?"

"I...forgive me," she whispered.

Mark shook his head, cold chills racing up and down his spine. "No, *chérie,* you are right. The problem is, how does one let go of the past and go on?"

Leah paused again. "I wish I knew."

Mark found that statement interesting. "Perhaps only day by day?" he suggested. "And with God's help?"

She nodded.

"I will make a pact with you. You pray for me every day and I will pray for you and at the end of the month we'll compare notes."

Leah chuckled. "It sounds like a deal."

She had unintentionally confirmed what he had suspected. Something in her past was what had pushed her to come out here and it still haunted her. He didn't let on what she had revealed, however. Instead he grinned and said, "So let me drive you home and set the tongues of Hill Creek to wagging."

Her laughter rang out, enchanting him. "I'd love it."

Gathering her purse, she pulled out money for her own meal. Mark stayed her hand and tossed down money for both of them. "Make no mistake, *chérie,* this was a date tonight and I am paying."

At the look of surprise on her face over his statement he decided she was definitely not used to going out. He was going to enjoy pampering her and teaching her the customs all over again. "But first," he added, grinning, "I think I want a sundae for dessert."

Leah groaned.

Mark chuckled. "And while we're waiting on that I'd like to tell you all about my 'artistic' abilities."

Seeing her attention refreshed and interested, he thought he was going to enjoy the rest of the night chatting with her. Giving up being a police officer would be worth it to be with her. It had to be. It *would* be.

Chapter Nine

"I'm glad you're considering Rebecca for this trip. She and Mom are so excited."

Leah smiled at Freckles and motioned for the young woman to come in. "Becca is a wonderful child. I'll get you that information. Come on in." Walking across the room to an old rolltop desk, Leah asked, "So, tell me, Freckles, how are you feeling today?"

Glancing over her shoulder she saw Dr. Susan McCade make a face. "Hawk made me go to a local obstetrician since my morning sickness had gotten so bad. It figures I'd wait until nearly the seventh month to start showing bad signs of morning sickness. I never do anything normal. Anyway, he prescribed something so *now* I am doing much better."

Leah laughed as she reached out to pull open her drawer where she'd stored all the information about the outing. Her laugh turned into a gasp as she grabbed her right shoulder.

"Hey, are you okay?" Freckles asked, coming forward, her doctor mode now in full forward motion.

Leah winced. "I've been practicing shooting a rifle, I'm afraid, and the rifle doesn't like me very much."

Freckles nodded wisely. "Why not allow me a quick look while I'm here?"

"Oh, no, Susan, I don't want to take advantage of you like that. It's just a bruise."

Freckles grinned. "You aren't taking advantage. Believe me, Hawk has been watching me like... well, like a hawk. He's really worried over this morning sickness so a small break from him isn't too bad. Come over here and sit down."

Leah opened her mouth to object, but Freckles grabbed her elbow and prodded her toward the dining room chair by the formal dinner table. She had learned not to argue. The entire town thought she was helpless.

Leah sat and patiently unbuttoned the pink top she wore.

"How is Mark treating you, by the way?"

Freckles said as she peeled back the top to study Leah's shoulder.

"Fine. I'm learning a lot from him."

"This shoulder is swollen and slightly blue. Looks like the joint is inflamed as well as bruised. We can write you up a prescription for that. Turn your arm for me," Freckles said and started rotating Leah's arm, to Leah's acute discomfort. "Yeah, that looks like all it is. I'll call something in to the pharmacist later. Now, about those lessons..."

Leah motioned Freckles to take a seat and passed her the paperwork. "As I said, they're going fine. We've had two lessons now."

"More than two lessons caused that shoulder problem," Freckles said cheerfully.

Leah sighed. "I've been practicing on my own."

"Is that safe?" Freckles asked, her smile turning to a frown.

"Probably not, but then, I'm not completely helpless and I wanted to impress Mark."

Freckles's eyebrows shot up and her eyes widened.

Leah shifted. "It's not like that, Freckles."

"I heard you two had dinner two nights ago at the café."

Leah sighed. "As a matter of fact, we did."

Freckles grinned. "I'm glad."

Oh, dear. Leah knew that smile. Freckles was about to launch into something.

"Mark is a good person. Julian and I have really gotten to know him since he's lived out on the ranch with us. He loves God but is wary of depending totally on Him. I suppose that's because of his past. Laura has mentioned that they didn't have the best childhood. Her mother died young and their father was a police officer who wanted his son to choose the same career. But Mark, seeing how he was left to Laura to raise and rarely seeing his father, rebelled against that lifestyle. Now, I see it this way. If you two are really dating like rumors have it, you'll have to be really careful about lying to him, which of course, I know you won't do, and not showing up when you say you will. This was a huge problem from his father—"

"It's not that serious!" Leah broke in flushing at the fount of information that Freckles was giving her. "To be honest," Leah began and found herself clasping her hands and trying to find a way to say this gently, "he's...tired of being matched up, as am I and we both thought if we dated...er...um...went places together that people would leave us alone."

Wincing at how blunt that sounded, but hoping to stop Freckles from revealing all of Mark's secrets to her—no matter how interested she might be—Leah looked to see how Freckles was taking the interruption.

Quite well, if the Cheshire cat grin was any indication. "If that's what you believe," Freckles chirped out. "Only time will tell."

Leah nearly groaned.

"You have a stabling influence on whoever you're around, Leah. I've always liked you and admired you. You're just shy and standoffish with most folks, and I guess it's because you're an only child...."

Leah shook her head. "I had a fine childhood, Freckles. Don't worry, I'm not going to hurt Mark if that's what you're worried about. My parents had me late in life and they doted on me until I married my childhood sweet—"

Leah gasped.

Freckles paused in glancing over the material to meet Leah's eyes. "You were married?"

Pain lanced through Leah as she realized what she'd given away. What to say? How to stem the flow of questions?

Honesty, she supposed. To a point. "Yes," she whispered. "At one time. He died a few years ago."

Surprisingly enough, Freckles didn't pursue that line of questioning. Instead, she reached out and squeezed Leah's hand. "I'm sorry. That's a hard loss. It's time you get back out with the living, Leah, and I'll leave it to you to set your own pace."

Leah smiled her thanks.

"Now about this program. Is there anything else besides this we have to do for Becca?"

Shaking her head, Leah replied, "Simply make sure she gets her physical and list any and all medications she's had in the last three months and anything else pertinent, like seizures. And make sure to get it to me in the next two weeks. I'm so glad your mom changed her mind about allowing Becca to go on the trip."

"It took some convincing, but when I promised to go along as the doctor with the group she caved in. I can't believe how excited she is now that she's given in to the idea."

"I imagine doing something like this is a big step for many of the parents."

Freckles nodded. "Becca has spent most of her life inside with one of us. I think the way she's flourishing since we've been out here is what finally swayed Mom."

"Well whatever it was, I'm glad. That's all I'll need. When I get the final paperwork I'll be sure to get a copy out to you."

"Thanks." Freckles stood. She padded across

the floor toward the front door. Once there she paused to pick up her bag. "You have no idea, Leah, how gifted you are with children. The gentle spirit you have about you is something I can only aspire to." Freckles smiled. "I just want you to know that if I've been too pushy with you it's simply because you bring out that caring instinct in people. They see the gentleness and mistake it for weakness. But I have a feeling you're much, *much* stronger than any of us have given you credit for."

With a quick smile Freckles pulled open the door. "Keep Mark in line."

That fast she was gone.

Leah didn't get a chance to respond but sat down, exhausted after Freckles's whirlwind visit. The woman never slowed down. She had to wonder if her pregnancy would slow her any.

She also talked a lot.

Freckles was the sweetest woman on Earth, but she had a problem about blurting out things she shouldn't. It wasn't that she was vicious or mean, but she spoke what was on her mind without thought. Leah had heard her do it several times. They often laughed about it together, but people here didn't know Leah had been married before. And if that slipped...

Leah twisted her hands.

She'd had a wonderful time the other night with

Mark. They'd gone to the café and eaten and ended up talking three hours. Meli had finally turned some of the lights out to hint she was closing before either one had realized how late it was.

They'd talked, of all things, about art. Not Monet or such, but kid's art. Finger painting and stick art, the things she did with the kids in school. Evidently the kids out on the ranch loved to get Mark to help them with such projects since Freckles had explained to them that he was an artist.

Before she'd known it, it was black out and the café was closing. Mark had driven her home and then gotten in his Jeep and left.

She'd lain in bed the rest of the night, sleepless, playing over the date again and again and wondering how, after all this time in town together and hardly ever speaking two words, the two of them could sit down and talk like they'd known each other forever.

Only her husband had been like that with her—and that was because they'd grown up together. Neighbors basically.

She had never expected to find someone she could talk to like that again—someone she thought she could trust.

Of course, she'd thought that about her husband and look where it'd gotten her.

But she had been young and naive then. She was

older and wiser now—and she missed the companionship.

"Father, I don't know what to do. I can't believe how nice it's been sitting and talking with Mark. I've just met him but I feel like I've known him forever. I'd love to get to know him better...but what about my past? What about my secret? If I ever decided to go deeper with a relationship, my past would have to come out. My name, my life, everything. That would mean exposing myself. If I'm exposed, then I'm vulnerable. Dan won't rest until he finds me. I have the book."

Leah rubbed her hands over her face. "I can't ruin my husband's reputation. I just can't. It wouldn't matter that he had been about to give it up. He'd be ruined. I'm not even sure...would I have to pay back the life insurance? Would I be held accountable because I had the book and didn't turn it over? I don't have the concrete proof, except that the book shows meetings. But that's still enough. How would I explain to Mark and the sheriff what they hear isn't the truth? What do I do? I've been running for years now, hidden from the nest of vipers I left behind. I need Your guidance, Your wisdom in this, Father. I wish, oh, how I wish Father, I could forget it, but You won't let me. So tell me, Father, what am I to do?"

The ruffling of the curtains as a gentle morning

breeze blew in was the only answer she got. That was because she already knew what she should do...but she wasn't ready. She couldn't go to the police and tell them what she knew. If she did, Dan would find her, and then...

She shuddered.

In this instance, she just couldn't do what her heart told her. She couldn't tell Mark the truth.

Dropping her head to the table she wondered what she was going to do.

Chapter Ten

"Did you hear me, Mark?"

Mark glanced over at Sherri. "Yeah, *chérie*, I was just working on this fence here though and—"

"You were not. You were staring off into space again."

Mark noticed the way the young girl pouted and the way she looked at him, which only brought his mind back to Leah again. She was right about Sherri. The young girl did have a crush on him. Taking a deep breath he sighed. "My mind was on Leah, Sherri," he admitted and offered her a tentative smile. "I'm helping her out with a project, and we've been spending time together over it."

Sherri's gaze cut away and she fidgeted. "I

don't see why she needs so much help. Maybe I could help her instead. I know the land just as well as you do."

Mark turned and rested an arm on the fence. "You do, but I'm enjoying my time with Leah, Sherri. However, I bet she'd let you come along as a guide later on if you still want to help," he offered gently, not quite sure how to handle the situation.

The sound of a truck coming down the road drew both of their attention briefly. Finally, Sherri sighed. "I suppose so. It's the sheriff coming this way. I wonder if Angela came with him."

"I hear she's dating a nice young man now," Mark added with emphasis on the word *young*.

"Yeah. She doesn't come out here much because of that."

"I saw Jeremy glancing at you the other day at church."

Sherri shrugged. However, he saw a hint of interest in her eyes. "He's dating someone else," she muttered.

"I don't know about that, but..." He paused as Mitch pulled up near them and killed the engine. When the sound died down, he continued, "I do know he has offered to help with some of the flyers for Leah. You might call him and tell him I suggested you help him."

Sherri's nose went up in the air. "I don't need anyone to fix me up, Mark." Miffed, she turned and stalked off, right past Mitch.

With eyebrows raised, Mitch walked on over to where Mark stood. "What'd you say to her?"

Mark shook his head. "I suggested she call Jeremy and help him."

Mitch chuckled. "I'm glad I don't have any children that age."

"She's not a child," Mark muttered.

Mitch nodded. "Julian has his hands full. He's taking these kids seriously, as if they were stepchildren instead of nieces and nephews. I would have never dreamed he'd be such a family man."

"Speaking of kids, how is your stepdaughter doing?"

Mitch grinned. "She has started calling me Daddy." Sticking his chest out he stuck his hands in his pockets. "And she's real excited that she's going to have a brother or sister soon."

Mark rolled his eyes. "The whole town is going to double in population if you McCades don't back off on the birth rate."

Mitch chuckled again. "What can I say? Our women love us."

"So, what's up?" Mark asked, pointedly ignoring Mitch's words.

"I was looking for Leah. I thought she might be out here."

"Here?"

Mitch nodded. "You two are working together. By the way, how's that going?"

Mark turned back to the fence where he was tightening the bolts. "Fine. I've enjoyed it. It's a nice break from what I was doing."

"But…?" Mitch prodded.

Mark growled low. "You know what. I've been by the office every day."

"You know, Mark, giving in to what you enjoy doesn't mean you're going to turn out like your father."

Mark spun around. "Oh? And how can you be so certain? He was a police officer, had it running in his veins! He loved the job. He ate it, slept it and talked it. You name it, he did it, if it had to do with his job. Even our vacations."

"Well, I'd say you were dedicated, but that much…" Mitch tried to joke.

Mark slumped back against the fence. "I'm not sure I can do it, Mitch. I vowed to quit. I want to work but if I meet the right woman, I don't want things to turn out like they did with my mom and dad."

"Maybe the right woman won't mind having a police officer as a husband. Maybe the right woman, Mark, will understand that on occasion, in a place like this, you might be called out. After all, this isn't New Orleans. You're not going to be working the hours they'd have there. Maybe the right woman just might not care as long as she had you.''

Mark thought of Leah. "Oh yeah, she would."

Mitch's gaze snapped sharply catching Mark's attention. He nearly groaned over what he'd said. Instead of confronting him bluntly, Mitch turned and rested a foot on the fence. "I heard you and Leah are being seen around town a lot together, especially since dinner the other night."

Well, he should have known he couldn't keep it from Mitch. "We thought it'd keep people off our backs about dating," he said and realized only then how lame that sounded.

"Yeah, right," Mitch snorted. "Tell me another one."

Mark slapped the wrench in his hand. Turning and taking the same pose as Mitch, he stared out across the green field where some of Zach Mc-Cade's cattle roamed in the far distance. "I don't know what I feel. How long have you known Leah?"

Mitch shrugged. "Leah's hard to know. She's distant, quiet, and stays away from most public events. Still, I was here when she moved out here and she has opened up some.''

"She's opened up? I find that hard to believe."

"Why?" Mitch prodded.

"I can't put my finger on it. She's skittish yet knows judo. She's—"

"Judo?"

Scowling at the disbelief in Mitch's voice, Mark said, "Yes. Judo."

"Who told you that falsehood?" Mitch asked shaking his head in disbelief. "I doubt the woman can stand the site of vio—"

"She took me down when I tried to scare her."

Mitch's jaw dropped open—just before he burst into laughter.

"She didn't?"

"Stop that laughing, *mon ami,* before I show you just what she did."

Mitch worked to contain his mirth. Finally he waved a hand. "I won't ask. Go on. How else is she a contradiction?"

"I don't know. She's leery about her past, especially anything to do with where she's from. I've seen that on several occasions. Have you ever noticed how she is when she's out and people are around? I mean, she's loosened up and been talking to me, but that only makes it more obvious. When someone that she doesn't know gets near her she clams up, drops her gaze to avoid conversation...." Mark jerked his hat off and ran a hand through his hair. "I don't know what it is that she does, but I do know she is bothered."

Hearing his own accent, Mark slapped his hat back on his head and grabbed a toothpick, slipping it into his mouth.

Mitch, knowing him so well immediately sensed his stress. "I don't know much about her, but if that's all that's bothering you, why not check over at the school and find out more about her? You are still officially part of my office, after all. My guess, after being in the business for a while, isn't a good one."

Mark nodded. "The way she is around men, especially you..."

"If I had to make a guess, I'd say she was assaulted in her past. It would explain her avoidance of men."

Mark shook his head. "I thought about that, but she doesn't seem leery of me."

"Maybe the self-defense gave her confidence." Mitch shrugged. "Give her time. Don't push her. Sometimes women need space to heal from things before they'll talk."

Mark saw the distant look enter Mitch's eyes and knew he was thinking of Suzi and the man who had been the father of her child. It had taken

Mitch a long time being a close friend with Suzi before she'd ever admitted to the mistake she'd made. Mitch still blamed himself for that mistake, Mark knew. He hoped and prayed his friend would soon let go of that pain.

"I'm really lucky, Mark. I have the greatest wife in the world—and an instant daughter." The pain left his eyes and he focused on Mark. "A good wife, friend or even woman to date is worth waiting for. If you enjoy Leah's company, allow God to lead you. Be patient, and when you feel the time is right, tell her about your past, your own worries about marriage—if it ever comes to that. One thing Suzi and I have learned is no more secrets. And I think that's going to make the difference with us."

Mark had to agree. "I've noticed Freckles has no secrets from your brother, either. Nor does Julian, though he's not quite as loud at expressing them."

Mitch chuckled. "I love that sister-in-law of mine. She's priceless." Mitch grinned. "Both of them. Yep, the McCade men made out lucky."

Mark frowned, realizing they had never gotten around to why Mitch needed to see Leah. "You said you were looking for Leah?"

"Yeah. I got some permits for her. I was knocking off early today and wanted to drop them by. Since I was on my way out here, and she wasn't at her house, I thought I'd bring them with me. Can you see she gets them?''

"Sure." Mark wouldn't mind an excuse to go into town later and talk with Leah. His mind had been on her all day and he'd found trying to do work around the ranch totally useless.

Mitch reached into his shirt pocket and pulled out some folded papers. "She's been waiting on these. Since school is out and the secretary was gone, they were left at my office."

"Small towns," Mark said.

"Yeah. They sure are nice. Well, now that I have that out of the way, I think I'll go visit my little brother and his wife before heading on home. Take care, Mark."

Mark nodded. "You, too."

Mark idly flipped through the permits thinking about the conversation he and Mitch had just had. Did Mitch realize Mark really was considering Leah for more than just a casual dating partner? He didn't want to admit to himself that it might be possible, but...

The memory of his mother, sitting at home, ruined dinners because his dad hadn't shown up and hadn't called to let her know wafted back to him, and he frowned. He believed to this day what really killed his mom was a broken heart.

He wasn't going to do that to anyone.

And he wasn't going to let his dad's environment rule his life.

With determination, he shook off his melancholy and headed toward his Jeep, intent on getting away from the cloying thoughts.

Chapter Eleven

"So this is what you wanted those permits for."
Scanning the map of the area he'd sketched out for
her, Mark shook his head. "This isn't going to
work."

"Of course it will." Leah moved over beside
him and dropped down onto the sofa, her pink
slacks and white shirt making her look fresh and
soft like the roses blooming out in front of her
house.

Mark couldn't help but notice, the entire time he
was arguing with her.

"See?" she said, pointing one long delicate finger at the map. "We can stop here for lunch. And
then the small area we are having built out there
with Mrs. Culpepper and the Sheriff's permission

to make it handicapped accessible will be perfect
to end up over here.'' She pointed to another area.

Shaking his head, he argued, ''That's not the
point, Leah.'' He was finding that the woman
could be stubborn when it came to what she
wanted. ''I'm sure that this would work perfectly
with the ramp you convinced them to build over
the gully. That is, if you wanted to spend an extra
day out there. We're going to have to cut the trail
you've laid out in half.''

''I don't think so.''

''How fast can someone in braces travel?'' he
asked bluntly.

Leah paused. ''Well, in school—''

''We won't be in school, *chérie*. We're going to
be out on the trail—a rough trail. Now, I agree
with your idea, letting them see the flora and fauna
of the area, sitting around a campfire for a night,
but this short two-day route you've mapped out
won't work for a kid in braces. You'll have to take
more breaks, slow down the walking and add more
to your program as you go to take up time for the
added delay.''

Leah's chin went up, surprising Mark.

''How can you be so sure you're right?'' she
asked.

''How can you be so sure *you're* right?'' he
countered.

Consternation flashed in Leah's eyes. "We're at a draw, it seems, Mark."

"Any of the kids that are going to be there in braces live here in Hill Creek?" he asked.

Leah shook her head. "No. And the only one in a wheelchair will be Becca."

"I don't think your wheelchair is going to be the problem," Mark offered now. "That's more stable than legs and canes. I honestly think, though, we need to make sure about this before you go ahead and submit this plan."

"But how?"

"I don't—"

"Wait!"

Mark blinked. "Okay, *chérie,*" he said causing her to blush.

"I meant, I have an idea. Since the hospital is one of our sponsors for this event perhaps they'd be willing to lend us some leg braces and we could test it out on our own."

Staring at her, he had to admit it was a good idea. He'd make sure to get his point across that way. He was certain he or Leah could walk that with no problem, but a bunch of kids, on braces— he just wasn't so sure. "Who would you contact?"

"The administrator. Wait here."

Leah jumped up and rushed toward the kitchen. Mark watched her go, thinking that was the most

animated he'd ever seen her. She had certainly relaxed around him since they'd been going out in
the evenings for dinner. They discussed the plans,
the map, had gone out scouting a large area…and
Leah, when involved in her work, had let down
her guard and was a different person.

At the café she still kept her voice down and
avoided others. Mark had thought long and hard
about what Mitch had said and had decided to give
his advice a try. He would be patient with Leah,
not push her.

He would find out her likes and dislikes, and
when he thought the time was right, he'd talk to
her about his dad and sister and what things had
been like. If he was serious about actually spending
time with this woman in a personal way, she deserved to know what baggage he carried around
with him.

And hopefully she'd confide in him, too.

Glancing around the room he saw the pink roses
on the coffee table, smelled the fresh scent and
thought again how innocent Leah looked. Getting
up he crossed to the bookshelves and ran a finger
over the books. Shakespeare, Byron, Shelley, Mil-
ton…the list went on. He saw a copy of a book
called *Little Men* and had no idea there had been
more in the series to one of his sister's favorite
books.

Moving along he continued reading off the names of classic authors until he came to a closed door. Opening it, not thinking really about what he was doing, he glanced to see what other types of books she read and was surprised to find books that his father had once owned.

Technical books regarding police work.

He gaped.

All kinds of familiar books were stacked one on top of the other. Unbelieving and just a bit too curious for his own good, he reached out to touch them. He tried to decide what quiet, shy Leah would be doing with such technical books.

To the side of the books were four small spiral notebooks, much like his sister had carried, like Mitch carried, like he carried.

Like almost every officer he ever knew carried. They were simple books for writing down information, a place to organize your thoughts, things you might have seen, information for later use in questioning.

Had Leah been a police officer?

Incredulously he picked one up, unable to rectify that image with what he was seeing now.

Well-worn, the dark-green cover curled on the edges, the corners white from use.

He opened the book, flipping it to the first page. *RH*—5/17/90. Initials. Not Leah's...

Quickly flipping the page, he scanned the contents. Three words jumped out at him, Dan, drugs and ongoing. *Scotlandville* jumped out at him. Why did that sound familiar? And...

Flipping back to the first page, he started to peruse more closely.

"I just called and— What are you doing?"

Mark turned, then realizing what he held in his hand, he quickly closed the book and dropped it back in the bookcase. He prayed she hadn't realized he'd actually read any of the books.

Leah stood there, pale, staring, her eyes wide, trying to see past the cabinet door to where his hand still rested.

Mark quickly closed the cabinet door, flushing to his hairline. "I'm sorry, *chérie,* I didn't mean to pry."

"You didn't have a right to go in there."

Actually, he was dying to know why, but he would not ask her now.

Leah shook her head then wilted into a nearby chair.

"I—they aren't mine, exactly."

Mark didn't believe that. At least, he didn't think he did. What was it about this woman that made him want to believe every word she said? Going over he dropped down on the sofa next to the chair she sat in. "You don't have to explain to me, *chérie*. I grew up with books like that in my house. My father was a police officer."

"No. I have to tell you. I mean..."

When she trailed off, he added awkwardly, "Leah, no. You don't have to."

"They were my husband's."

Had Mark not been sitting he would have been after that announcement. "Your *husband?*"

"Ex-husband. No, not ex. I'm not divorced." She started wringing her hands

"You're not divorced!" Mark stood, shocked down to his toes, unable to believe what she'd just said.

Her gaze snapped up to his. "Oh, dear." Distressed she shot to her feet. "No, that's not what I meant. He's dead!"

Mark fell back down into his chair. "Dead?"

"He died in the line of duty years ago, and I really don't talk about it..."

He grabbed her hands to stop the wringing. Pulling her back down to the chair, for only then did he realize he was sitting, he said, "It's okay. Forgive me, *chérie,* I did not know."

Squeezing her hands, he waited until she lifted her pain-filled gaze to his. "I am from a family of police officers, *chérie.* I understand the life. And I understand putting the pain in the past and going onward."

A small voice whispered in his heart, *Then why haven't you let go of your own pain?* Mark winced.

"I am sorry to have brought up painful memories."

Leah shook her head. "No. It's all right. I'd been trying to think how to bring up the subject. It's not one I've spoken of since moving here. And I thought you should know since Freckles knows."

Susan knew? He tried not to let her see his surprise. "She certainly wouldn't mention something like that to me, especially if you told her patient to doctor or even friend to friend. I had no idea. I'm sorry for your loss."

"It's been a few years. It seems like a lifetime sometimes. While other times, when I see you or Mitch or something else that triggers it, it feels like just yesterday."

Aha, he thought. That was why she didn't like the police.

He pushed those thoughts from his mind to concentrate on Leah's pain right now. "That is how death is," he murmured softly. "Do you want to talk about it?"

Leah shrugged. "Yes and no. But I need to."

He simply waited.

"We married young. He was my childhood sweetheart. It just seemed right to marry." Glancing at him, she let out a shaky breath. "We were just so young. I had no idea what life was. Neither did he.''

Glancing at the flowers, she drifted from him. He could feel it. Her mind slipped back to another time. ''We were in love as much as a young person can understand love. That silly feeling of attraction and the feeling you are starting out on a grand quest, that you've got the world in front of you and nothing can stop you.''

A sad smile touched her lips. ''Almost immediately I knew Bobby wasn't happy. No, that's not right. He was happy, but restless. He loved his job but wanted more. He was a good man. He spent a lot of time at the station and quickly got promoted. And then spent more time, and more time and time in the evenings. It got to where he wasn't home. I took up gardening. I love to grow things. We drifted until—'' she hesitated ''—I became pregnant. Bobby was ecstatic. We wanted to make our marriage something more so we decided to move away from the big city and start over. Six days later, Bobby was…killed…in the line of duty.''

Mark listened to her story without moving. Finally, he reached out and slipped an arm around her, hugging her gently. ''I'm sorry, Leah.''

''Two months later I miscarried. I came out here to start over. I had thought to just let the past be the past but...since someone else knew, I didn't want you hearing the truth from them.''

The truth. What an odd way to put it, he thought. "Your past is just that, *chérie*. It is your past. We all have pain we bring with us.

"My father was a police officer and I watched as his dedication to duty and his obsession with being the best killed my mother. Being the wife of a police officer is a hard life.''

Leah nodded. "Sometimes.'' But as she sat there, with Mark hugging her, she had a stray thought that being the wife of this part-time police officer wouldn't be bad at all. "But to be honest, I didn't mind it. It is simply a different way of life.''

Mark heard her words and for some reason felt a small opening bud of peace bloom up within him.

Pulling back she grabbed a tissue from the holder on the small table and dabbed at her eyes. "Forgive me, Mark. I guess the shock of seeing you find those books... I wasn't prepared.''

Mark rubbed a hand over his eyes. "You have no need to apologize, *chérie*. I was gauche, doing something I should have thought twice about. Please don't apologize again.''

Leah nodded, relieved to have that off her mind. Finally! She had wanted to tell Mark—especially since she had been enjoying his company so much of late. But how to tell him had been the question. Seeing him over in the cabinet where she kept her private books—including her husband's old log-book, she had felt her stomach drop with shock.

The story—more than she had wanted to come out—had spilled at his feet. She was embarrassed now having told him that she and her husband had actually had problems. She was certain she and Bobby would have eventually worked them out since neither one believed in divorce but…to tell someone else about that, someone that she wasn't really close to…

Suddenly she realized she must be closer than she thought if she was so willing to share such a thing with Mark.

"So what did the hospital say, Leah?" Mark asked.

Leah smoothed her shirt, pulling her thoughts back in line. "Oh, they said we could check out two sets of braces for the day. I told them we'd be over to get them shortly."

"Did you tell them what they were for?"

Leah, feeling much better, relaxed and nodded. "And they were more than happy to help out. Do you want to go with me to test them or would you rather meet later?"

Mark studied her a moment then touched her hand. "You did not scare me off, sweetheart. So, please, let's forget it. As I said, we all have baggage, wounds in various stages of healing. As you know, God chooses different ways to heal them and different times for each of us."

"I'm glad you were listening Sunday," Leah quipped and stood. "Let me get some water and then we can leave."

"We can go from there over to Mrs. Culpepper's for the dinner tonight," he called out after her.

Leah wondered about that and how she would fit in.

One thing was certain, she was more than fitting in with Mark. She couldn't deny how attracted she was to him, or how much she enjoyed his company. But she couldn't get involved with the law.

But if he was really thinking about leaving it...

Chapter Twelve

"I had no idea this was so hard."

Mark agreed. "I think I'm going to have blisters."

Leah paused with her crutches and braces and glanced back toward Mark, who was just behind her. Her hair was hanging down in tendrils around her face, her cheeks flushed, her nose scrunched up against the late-afternoon sun. "Just how long has it been that we've been tracing this trail in these things?"

"At the distance we've made and the area you want to cover, it would take us nearly three days to cover it."

He wasn't lying.

Leah groaned.

Mark agreed. "We have to take into consideration the children are much more used to these than we are. So still, at the fastest we might travel, it would be a day and a half."

Leah hobbled over toward a boulder and went to sit down. Mark followed. Instead of sitting down she lost her balance and fell, headlong to the ground.

Mark jumped to intercept her and ended up in a tangle on the ground with her.

"I'm so sorry," Leah said, rolling to her back and sitting up.

"If only that had been under better circumstances," he teased and sat up, too. He reached down and quickly released his braces.

Turning, he worked to help Leah.

"You were right, you know."

Her soft voice, the way she admitted to him that he had guessed right caused a warmth to swell up within his heart. "I think you underestimated the distance is all, *chérie*," he offered.

Setting the brace aside, he stood and offered her his hand.

She reached up and allowed him to pull her to her feet. Stretching, he watched as Leah dusted herself off and then smoothed her top before pinning the loose strands of her hair back up.

"Are you always so tidy?" Mark asked.

The wind blew lightly. It always blew, Mark had realized not long after moving here. The dust kicked up and the leaves rustled. All else was quiet except for an occasional hawk calling out.

Surprised, Leah glanced up. "Tidy?"

Mark reached out and touched a tendril of hair. "This doesn't detract from your looks," he said.

Leah's cheeks brightened with a pink flush. "It's supposed to go with the rest of the hair."

Mark shook his head. "Not necessarily, *chérie.*"

Leah's eyes traced his features before skittering away. Clasping her hands, she turned and moved back to where she'd laid the leg brace. She began gathering the pieces together. "I think what we'll do is break earlier for lunch and then at the other point where we were going to stop for lunch, we can bed down for the night. If we use the next day to cut directly west instead of going on up northward, that should work for our route."

Mark had seen interest in Leah's eyes before she'd turned away. Interest and a certain wariness. Instead of turning him away though, that wariness made him want to hold her, offer to protect her from whatever it was that had put that fear in her eyes.

Before he'd done any such thing, she'd gathered her thoughts and trotted off in another direction to give herself space.

"I think that would work fine, Leah." He liked the way her name sounded. And he had found, being around her the last couple of weeks, that Leah certainly wasn't scatterbrained or unable to take care of herself as he'd first thought.

Today as they'd walked the trail in the metal contraptions, he'd watched as she'd determined where she was going. Nothing was going to stop her. Only a strong woman could do that, someone who knew what she wanted and went after it.

She was nothing like he'd thought she would be when they'd first met. He'd thought a woman like her surely would have complained about the scraped hands or bruises from their fall.

Instead, she'd pulled herself up and gone on.

Mark found he had thoroughly enjoyed his time with her. Each day he was finding more and more pleasure just being around her and discovering what type of woman she was.

She was a jewel.

Not something overstated but something quiet, serene, something like an opal that had hidden qualities in it if you only took time to look.

"What are you staring at?"

Mark blinked, realizing he had been staring. "At you, *chérie,*" he admitted honestly. "I was thinking you are much stronger than I gave you credit for. Indeed, much stronger than anyone in the town gives you credit for.''

He enjoyed the way her pale cheeks tinted up with another light flush. She glanced away. ''I'm not that strong. My arms are killing me after what we just did.''

''So are mine,'' Mark replied, smiling as he set about gathering up his own equipment. ''However, that is not what I meant. I meant inner strength. I see now why you teach. Only someone who could spend hours doing what we have done today could handle a class of kindergartners.''

Leah chuckled. ''You're making too much of it.''

Mark started back down the trail with Leah at his side. ''I don't think so. I also think I owe you another apology for doubting you.''

Leah shrugged, obviously not comfortable with all the attention. ''Life is a lesson of learning. Things you saw in me that you perceived as weak might have been wrong. However, let's not forget I didn't know how to shoot a rifle. Nor did I know to bring a cell phone with me while out on the range like this.''

''True. But you were willing to learn.''

''And I thank you for teaching me,'' she replied lightly.

Mark admitted to himself that she would go no

further with this conversation, so he changed the subject. "Tell me why you haven't come out to Mrs. Culpepper's before now."

Leah shrugged, not sure what to tell Mark. She'd enjoyed this afternoon so much with him and wasn't sure she wanted to be around a group of other people.

"I'm not really into large social gatherings. A few times I'd heard talk around church about get-togethers out on the ranch but..."

"But, as you say," Mark interjected in that deep, gentle voice of his, "you don't like large gatherings."

"That's right."

"So why are you going now?" he asked, his voice filled with a peaceful sound of pleasure.

She glanced up at him, grinning. "I didn't feel you'd given me much of a choice."

Mark chuckled, which sent a small thrill of anticipation down her spine. How was this man able to cause these feelings in her? she had to wonder.

She actually found she enjoyed the excitement of being with him...yet, she'd promised herself she wouldn't.

She knew it wasn't the need to tempt fate, which she surely was doing by getting close to him.

He was handsome, very handsome, she admitted. But so were the McCades and Tessa's husband, Drake, and many other men of Hill Creek.

She didn't find herself drawn to any of them like she was to this man.

What was it, then?

She admitted once again it had to be the fact that he actually acted as if he needed her. Where others saw only a helpless woman, he'd seen through that to the real Leah inside, the one who enjoyed teasing and liked to read, the woman who could be stubborn when the moment called for it, the woman who was lonely and missed having a life mate.

He saw that.

No one else ever had. She'd always been just Leah. The woman who needed to be watched, but nothing else.

"I will admit, Leah, that I am glad you are going tonight. Mrs. Culpepper is a lonely woman and goes all out when she has these fellowships. She loves having company. I feel guilty for not being over there more often."

"I never knew that about her," Leah murmured. "I see her occasionally in church but..."

"For some she is hard to get to know."

"I guess I have never made the effort," Leah confided and realized that was true. In the entire time she'd been in Hill Creek she had only gotten to know two or three people closely. All of the rest that she had met were just passing strangers.

"There's always time to correct that oversight," Mark said as the Jeep came into sight.

"I'm not sure if I'm ready," Leah murmured, suddenly worried as her past came up to haunt her.

Mark walked up to the vehicle and tossed the braces in and then reached for Leah's. Finally he turned and said, gently, "Take it one step at a time, Leah. Trust God to work out whatever problems you might find along the way."

Leah shifted and said, "Just like you will allow God to work out your problems?"

Mark actually grinned at her. "He's working on it, *chérie*. Since we talked I have realized I allowed my father to control too much of me. He is dead and will never come back. I should do what I want to do, without worrying whether he would have cared or not."

Surprised, Leah stared. "You decided that just from our conversation?"

His gaze touched her features. "That and more, *chérie*, but I don't think you are ready to hear the rest."

She swallowed, hard. "So, what have you decided?"

Mark's smile faded. "I don't know."

"You don't know?"

Mark shook his head. "All I know is that much of that guilt is gone. I've prayed and given it over to my God and now I must decide in which direction it is He wants me to proceed."

"Oh."

Mark shrugged, his smile returning. "I'm sure He'll show me. Maybe right now, I am just not ready to see it."

Leah well understood what he meant. Facing what God revealed within the hidden recesses was sometimes scary and nearly impossible. Though her heart told her it was the right thing to do, her mind argued, telling her that in the physical world too many things could happen that would spell disaster.

It all boiled down to trusting Him.

Could she?

As Mark seemed to be doing?

Could she, especially since she definitely was developing feelings for Mark? Though he didn't seem interested in the police force, he was still an officer of the law, and if she confided what she felt she should to him, he would be bound by his duty.

Quietly she followed him into the vehicle, willfully redirecting her thoughts to wonder just what Mrs. Culpepper's festivities would include.

Chapter Thirteen

When they drove up, the sun was starting its descent toward the western sky. Several cars, pickup trucks, and four-by-fours were parked in the driveway. Children were running around chasing each other, laughing and squealing. She saw one of her former students with a horned toad in her hands, chasing a boy.

Closer to the elongated two-story house, which was painted white with a pale-blue trim, Leah noted that there were speakers set up and music playing. A group of teens and young adults were standing around them, microphones in some of their hands, singing the latest Christian pop songs.

She saw one of the other people grab a microphone and join in.

Out in the yard, a group of adults sat and chatted. Toward the side of the house some were playing volleyball and others jumping on the trampoline.

Leah grinned, wondering what Mrs. Culpepper was doing with a trampoline.

"I have wondered about the trampoline myself," Mark murmured, reading her mind as they started toward the groups. Along the front porch were four tables, all filled with food. If she had learned one thing, it was that Christians sure could eat. Every time they got together, there was plenty of food.

"Look," Mark suddenly said and pointed. "Come, let's go talk with Wil."

Leah followed his gaze and saw Wil in the middle of a pile of wood, stacking it. "Bonfire?" she asked.

"They usually have one, though there's not a lot of wood to burn. Mainly it's what has been cleared off. They've spent the day watering down the area. When it gets later in the summer, they won't have bonfires."

"A waste of water," Leah agreed, knowing how dry it got out here. "And the risk of brush fire."

"Yeah. I've never been in one and hope never to see one of those that hits here every so often."

"I see you made it, young ones," Wil said dusting off his hands before pulling Mark into a hug and slapping his back.

"I told you we would," Mark said.

Wil grinned and stuck his hand out to Leah. "I knew you would. It is the woman whom I am happy to have here."

Snorting, Mark said, "You enjoy seeing all the women here."

Mrs. Culpepper chose that moment to hurry over, a lighter fluid container in her hands. "Here you go, Wil. This will help."

"That'll probably blow us up," Zach said strolling up from where he had just arrived, on horseback.

Leah glanced over and saw Laura as well, dismounting from Jingle Bells. Laura had her baby in a carrier strapped to her front, snuggled nice and close.

"She rode that horse all the way here?" Mark asked, surprised.

Zach grinned proudly. "She and her horse have finally made peace. As a matter of fact, she is the *only* one who can ride him."

"That is no horse, it's a monster," Leah said watching as Laura headed over toward the corral with her animal's reins in one hand and the other resting on the back of her child.

"He's a pussycat," Zach countered. Coming

forward he leaned down and kissed Mrs. Culpepper on the cheek and then pulled Leah into a gentle hug. "How you doing, schoolteacher?"

Leah smiled. "Fine. Just fine."

"We're so glad you made it," Mrs. Culpepper said. Her bright-silver curls showed her many years with their gray-and-silver streaks.

Leah nodded. "It's hectic, isn't it?"

Mrs. Culpepper, Leah noted, stood next to Wil, who had cocked one hip and leaned slightly toward her. "It sure is. But just wait until the hayride. Oh, the hayride. Wil, are you going to do the honors tonight? Or should we get Mark here to drive the tractor?"

"Tractor?" Leah asked.

Mrs. Culpepper giggled like a schoolgirl. "My, yes, Leah. We hook up the wagon to a tractor and drive it around the field. There's always a few people who want to experience it. It can be a really fun thing. We start the rides right after dark and have one every half hour for two hours so everyone gets a chance. The kids are most fond of it."

Leah relaxed at Mrs. Culpepper's exuberance. She liked the old woman very much. "It sounds lovely."

Mrs. Culpepper laughed again then shook a finger at Mark. "You go get her some punch or a soda. It's warm out here and she's flushed."

Laura came trotting over just as Mark replied, "Yes, ma'am."

"Hi," Laura said waving and going right to her husband. All of Zach's attention turned to the woman at his side. Reaching up, he ran a finger over his child's hair that poked up out of the cloth carrier, and cooed. Laura smiled at Zach and patted the baby's bottom as both became absorbed in the other.

Feeling that this was the best time to extricate herself from the conversation, Leah smiled again at Mrs. Culpepper. "Thank you. I think I'll take Mark up on that."

Mark simply lifted an eyebrow. "You liked my suggestion, eh?"

She couldn't help but laugh as she realized she'd given credit to Mark for the idea. She turned and they started toward the long screened-in porch where the food and beverages were set up. "I do believe Mrs. Culpepper suggested it."

Mark chuckled. "She likes to make sure all her guests know to make themselves at home. Tell me, what do you think of her in her own environment?"

"She's lovely. I think, though—" Leah hesitated.

"What?" Mark asked pulling the screen door open for her.

She passed through and turned to say quietly, "I think she may like your friend, Mr. Whitefeather."

A slow smile curved Mark's lips. "They think it's a well-kept secret, how they feel for each other. I imagine one day they'll finally confess."

"Oh?" Leah was all ears, excitement rising in her at the thought of Wil and Mrs. Culpepper together. "They would make a striking couple," she said thinking it over in her mind.

"Are all women matchmakers?" Mark asked wryly, as he filled a plastic cup with ice and handed it to her.

"I'm not a matchmaker," Leah protested, realizing that was exactly what she had been doing.

Mark's gaze fell and he said, softly, "Shucks, ma'am," which sounded totally absurd coming from his mouth, "And I thought maybe you might have a match in mind for me."

Leah's eyes widened in surprise.

Before she could reply, a man from church that Leah didn't know walked up and hit Mark on the back. His attention diverted from her, she watched him take the toothpick from his mouth and start joking.

And the entire time she had to wonder if he'd meant she had a match for him or that she just might be that match.

He might not have said it, but it had certainly crossed her mind.

"...if that's okay with you, Leah."

Leah's gaze jerked toward Mark. "Excuse me?"

He grinned. "I just told Judson that we were both too tired to join him in a game of volleyball. He's trying to get up a team. However, if you feel like you could do it..."

When he trailed off she shook her head. "Not at all. If you'd like to go ahead, Mark, please do."

He shook his head. "Sorry, Judson, but I have other things on my mind." His gaze never left her.

She felt the blood rush to her face.

"Okay, man," Judson said and with a turn, pulled open the door. "Later, maybe. Hey, anyone," he called out in general, "volleyball?"

Leah heard him but had been unable to break Mark's gaze, until the door slammed shut behind Judson. Jumping, she turned and plucked up a plate. Quickly filling it, she ignored the undercurrent of tension.

When Leah was done, she walked outside to a nearby table. She heard Mark directly behind her. Both seated themselves before Mark spoke again. "So, would you like to simply sit here and listen to the music, or mingle, or maybe a hayride later?"

"Too hot for a hayride," Leah murmured. "I'll leave that to the young children."

Mark grinned. "Fair enough. Then how about we just sit and listen?"

Leah bit into a chip she'd dipped in some guacamole. "Maybe we could walk down to the barn and see the horses. I wanted to look again at that horse Laura rode. I still can't believe it let her ride it."

"Jingle Bells can be pretty stubborn," Mark said grinning. "I've watched Laura struggle with her from the beginning. Jingle Bells dumped Laura at the fairgrounds, ran her under a tree trying to knock her off, and even dropped her in a creek..."

"So why did Laura keep bothering then?"

"She's stubborn."

Leah grinned. "I've seen that in her."

"I've seen that in you, too, *chérie.*"

Leah blinked. "I am not stubborn."

"It took getting you out on braces to convince you I was right."

"Which only proves you are stubborn," Leah retorted.

Mark snorted. "Me? How do you figure that?"

"You wouldn't take my word for it but had to prove me wrong." Leah grinned and then took another bite of chip.

Mark burst into laughter. "As I said, stubborn."

Leah smiled, warming at his pleasure. "When it's needed, I can be," she finally admitted.

"A life survival skill," Mark added.

Leah nodded. "Certain things require stubbornness, like faith."

Mark's smile dimmed a bit. "I suppose it does, doesn't it, *chérie?*"

Leah nodded though she thought that was one area she just wasn't stubborn enough in. She should simply believe and let go of her fears but...

"You want to go on that walk now?"

Leah glanced down and realized during their short conversation she'd devoured the chips. "Very well."

Standing, Leah pushed back her chair. Gathering her plate she hurried to the trash can and dropped it in.

Mark followed right beside her. He turned and headed toward the barn at a leisurely pace. The sound of laughter and shouting filled the air, good old-time fun as people joked and laughed and children played.

"It's been a long time since I've been involved in things like this."

"I have noticed you tend to keep to yourself if you show up at the church picnics," Mark murmured.

The orange of the setting sun cast shadows in the yard, causing Mark's face to appear softer than she knew it was. She liked the semidarkness. It gave a sense of isolation and comfort. If it had been lighter out she might not have been so chatty. But with the sun continuing its descent she found she could open up about things that she had long held secret.

"I do tend to stay to myself." She nodded, inhaling the fresh smell of lilies growing in the front yard. "I have found it's easier to stay focused if I'm not going in so many directions."

The sounds faded the farther they got from the group of people. "Yet you sacrifice friendship at that cost."

"Admittedly, it's a hard choice sometimes but—"

Leah paused and nibbled her lip as she tried to think how to hint at what she wanted to discuss.

"But friends can betray us," Mark said softly.

They arrived at the corral and Leah followed the fence to the adjacent barn. Leah trembled at Mark's words. "Yes. Experience?" she asked, curious as to how he could have guessed what she had been thinking about. Her husband and Dan had been close friends.

"Not really, *chérie.* I've never had a lot of close friends. I have many acquaintances but few real friends. I just know because of my father's betrayal. I sense that same distress in you, that same inability to let go and trust someone new."

Leah clasped her hands together. How did she explain to him it was more than that? She started down the aisle, studying the different horses as they walked.

It was quiet here, the scent of hay and horses strong. The only sound was the far-off noise of the party and the occasional scuffing of a horse's hoof. One snorted and shook its head while another shifted.

Overall, it was peaceful.

"You can talk to me, *chérie,* if you need to," Mark murmured.

Leah paused near the stall where Laura had settled her horse and stared at the animal. Defiantly the horse stared her in the eye, daring her to be brave, to be honest, to show the strength of character this horse had shown when she'd first met Laura.

A small still voice whispered in her heart to confide, to get rid of the past, to let it go. Exposing it would be the only way to break the power her past had....

"I—" Leah turned, hands still clasped at her waist.

Mark stood there, in front of her, his gaze intense, full of concern as he stared down at her. She could tell he worried about whatever bothered her.

The obvious regard in his expression told her he really wanted to help.

Could she do it?

"I'm...running, Mark. From—"

A horse's nose in her back knocked her off balance.

Leah gasped and flailed, attempting to catch her balance.

Mark leaped forward to grab her and their heads collided. "Ooomph."

With a grunt, Mark stumbled.

Leah, who tried to regain her balance, caught a foot on Mark's outstretched one. "Ahhgh!"

She felt herself falling. There was no way to avoid it. And in a flash of a second she realized she was going to land right on top of Mark.

Briefly she prayed she didn't hurt him too much.

And for the second time that day, she felt strong sure arms wrap around her and cushion her fall.

Chapter Fourteen

"We've got to stop meeting like this."

Leah groaned.

Mark chuckled, not really minding at all that he once again got to hold the soft feminine form within his grasp.

Leah shoved up to where she could see him, and Mark snickered. All he could see was a mass of blond hair covering her face.

"Stop laughing. That horse shoved me down!"

Mark only chuckled more. "She's a one-person horse," he quipped.

Reaching up he pushed her hair aside.

He had only intended to help her. But seeing the flushed look on her cheeks and the absolute spark of uncontrolled emotion—it touched off an answering spark deep within Mark. "I knew, *chérie,* that you covered up your emotions from many," he said softly, his gaze penetrating, seeking more within her, emotions she'd held in check until now.

And he found it. There, in her answering gaze was her own desire for him, a desire that reminded him of how long it'd been since he'd actually dated a woman—a real woman and not just a colleague with whom he had shared dinner over work.

Still holding her hair back, he turned his hand to where he cupped her cheek. Gently, carefully, allowing her to say no, he eased her forward inch by inch, until her lips were a mere hairbreadth away.

Once again he checked her gaze and found her eyes drifting shut. Leaning up he made contact. Her lips were soft, gentle, and lonely, he thought as he tilted her head slightly to deepen the kiss.

And he realized just how very lonely he was, and how very enchanted by this woman.

He discovered he was more than simply infatuated with Leah...it went way beyond simple attraction. His emotions were involved, his heart was involved.

Mark could actually imagine settling down....

Pulling back from the kiss, his eyes met hers again and they both simply stared at each other.

A snort from Jingle Bells had Leah scrambling off Mark—to his painful dismay.

Mark scooted backward and stood. Snatching up his hat, he dusted it off and then fished for a toothpick out of his pocket.

Leah had intertwined her fingers and stood there, not quite meeting his gaze.

"I apologize, *chérie,* if I did something inappropriate."

How had that happened? he had to question. They'd been walking, ended up in the barn and had been talking about something and then—

"No. I—I participated," she whispered.

Mark tilted his head, studying her. Reaching out, he caught her hand. "Is it so bad if you also enjoyed it?" he asked.

Leah nibbled her lip. Mark watched as she slowly pulled herself together. Finally she shook her head. "I guess…you're the first person I've gone out with or kissed since my husband's death," she finally admitted.

Ah… Mark thought. "Should I back off, then?"

He saw a struggle take place within her. Over what, he didn't know. But finally she shook her head. Reaching up, she pushed her disheveled hair back behind her ear. "No. I— Oh, Mark," she whispered again.

Mark pulled her into his embrace and just held

her. She trembled and Mark rubbed her back. Soon he felt tears wetting his shirt.

He didn't release her or question her, he simply continued to rub her back. Leah was a strong cedar of Lebanon, he thought, thinking of how those trees could be bent to the ground but not break while others might lie in ruin around them. A strong and mighty tree able to withstand the worst of storms.

How he knew this, he wasn't sure. Perhaps it was in her eyes.

He was glad that God allowed him to be here now, though, for this woman as she was bent under a burden from her past—under the grief, he assumed, of the loss of her husband.

Finally he opened his mouth and whispered a quiet prayer, words of comfort and exhortation and praise of their God, of what Jesus Christ had done for them, how He had died for them to take their burdens and to strengthen them until the day of His reappearing. Mark praised Him for that and praised Him that they would one day stand before Him and there would be no more pain.

He wasn't sure when, but somewhere along the way, Leah's tears finished and she had joined in praising Jesus and God their Father.

Mark felt His peace descend and wrap around them, isolating them from the turbulent world as

God did a work in his heart and, if he wasn't mistaken, Leah's life as well. Eventually they both fell quiet though they continued to stand there embracing each other.

Finally, he stepped back.

Leah glanced up. Her face had red splotches and her eyes were swollen.

Mark thought he'd never seen a more beautiful woman in his life.

"I must look a mess," she finally said and raised a hand to her cheek in embarrassment.

Mark caught her hand and leaned down. Pulling the toothpick from his mouth he tossed it aside. Then he placed a gentle kiss on the palm of her hand. "You look like a woman who has just been to the throne room and found an answer to a problem."

Leah nodded. "I have. He is truly a wonder," she added smiling.

Mark stepped back. "Do you want to go back to the party or do you want to go home?"

The tension was completely gone as they stood there facing each other. "Actually, you read my mind, Mark. I-if you don't mind..." she squeezed his hand and only then did he realize he still held it.

"Yes?" he asked, and released her hand.

"I'm exhausted from all we've done today. If

you wouldn't mind, would you drop me home and then tomorrow..."

She trailed off. Mark nodded. "Tomorrow we can talk more."

"Yes," she replied.

"Yes." He nodded. "Let's go say our goodbyes and then I'll take you home, Leah mine."

Leah blinked.

Mark liked the flush that came to her cheeks. One of his friends here often said that to his wife and Mark now understood why. That fit so well. That possessive feeling, the need to protect that came out when he'd discovered he had feelings for someone.

Love?

He wasn't sure.

Deep emotional need?

Most definitely.

How to handle it?

Prayer.

That was the only answer he could come up with. And he planned to do a lot of it once he got her home.

His entire world had just been shattered with the realization that he might not be single the rest of his life, that God possibly had other plans for him.

It was going to take a while for him to adjust to it and then decide what to do from there.

Leah had turned and with a very wary glance at the horse that had knocked her down, skirted around Jingle Bells and then headed for the barn exit.

Mark grinned at the horse and mouthed a silent thank you for its stubbornness and need to act out as he followed after Leah. He couldn't help thinking that horse might just be on his side as well.

They both said their goodbyes to Wil and Mrs. Culpepper and then headed to the Jeep. Once within the confines of the vehicle, Leah muttered, "That horse is a menace. I wonder how Zach didn't keep from selling her off."

Mark chuckled. "From what I understand, that was Angie's horse before it was Laura's."

Leah nodded. "You're absolutely right. I have no idea how that child managed to stay on that horse. She must be a master at it."

Leah thought about Zach's daughter and shook her head.

"Did you teach her in school?"

Glancing back at Mark she realized whatever had happened at the barn must be far from his mind now. Not for her it wasn't.

Her lips were still tingling from the kiss she had so wanted to experience. And here he was blithely talking about Zach's daughter. Of course, she *had* brought the subject up.

"I wasn't here when she was a student in the lower grades. I do know her, however. Everyone knows everyone in a small town, no matter how much of a recluse one might be."

Mark chuckled.

That chuckle didn't do anything at all for Leah's nerves. She trembled all over from the sound. She had known, though she'd fought it, that she was attracted to Mark.

But when he'd asked permission with his eyes to kiss her, had taken it so slowly so she could back away if she wanted—what type of man would do that?

Her pulse had raced and her heart ached as she'd suddenly realized that was what she wanted—his kiss.

And right in the middle of the kiss, she had realized that the reason she had yearned for it so much was that she had fallen in love with this man.

She didn't believe in love at first sight.

She believed a person had to know someone like she had known her husband—nearly all her life— to fall in love.

Love was more than simple emotions. It was a willingness to commit your entire life to someone, for better or worse. It was a covenant with God, a shadowing of the body of Christ. She knew how serious marriage was. It wasn't something based solely on a fluttering feeling and an impulsive decision to marry. She knew that by uniting with a man, she became one in spirit. The woman represented the church while the man represented Christ and God was at the head.

No one could feel the way she did, be willing to commit to something *that* serious in only a few weeks of close association.

But as he'd kissed her there in the barn she'd found herself thinking, *He's the one.*

The confirmation in her spirit said she was right.

But she couldn't be.

When he'd released her she'd cried.

How could she keep from it? The commitment she had thought about in her heart was something that would be impossible without telling the whole truth to this man.

As she'd stood there and cried she'd silently begged God for help.

Then Mark had started praying. In the spiritual realm she had felt the battle going on around them, not sure about what or why, but only that her answer was there and Mark's prayers were helping. Then, as clear as if she'd heard an audible voice, she heard in her spirit, *Get the evidence and give it to Mark.*

She'd known then she had no choice. She would

have to get the book and show Mark what she knew.

How could she not? She loved him....

Still stunned over what she'd admitted she sat there in silence as they drove.

Mark, obviously sensing her need not to talk, had dropped the subject of Angela.

It wasn't until they neared the town limits of Hill Creek that Leah finally spoke. "Thank you for tonight. I did enjoy it."

"Despite getting knocked down twice, and dusty and sweaty and..."

She laughed. As she did, she noted she felt freer than she had in years. "Yes. Despite all of that." Her laughter faded as she grew serious. "Mark, there is something I want to share with you. However, it'll be a week before I can reveal everything. Will you wait that long?"

Mark turned down the side street toward Leah's house. "If you feel a need to wait, *chérie,* I will give you all the time in the world."

They pulled up to her house and Mark killed the engine before getting out and coming around to her side of the vehicle. She was already half-out when he grabbed the door.

A twinkle in his eyes, he nodded toward her front door for permission.

She acknowledged her acceptance with a silent

tilt of her head. Then tentatively she reached out and touched his hand.

His warm hand, so large compared to her own, much rougher, and so very male, wrapped around her hand.

Contentment touched her bone-weary soul.

They strolled up the walk to the front door. Leah pulled out her key and opened it.

"Thank you, Leah, for tonight."

Leah walked in holding the door open. "Thank you, Mark."

She heard Mark follow her. "I have something I want you to read if you have time."

"I'd be glad to," Mark said.

She crossed to the closed cabinet and pulled it open, looking for her husband's small notebook.

"I'm not so sure you'll like it," she said softly. "It was...it was one of my husband's daily notebooks. I'd like you to get to know him," she finally said.

She picked up the notebook, so small it fit in the palm of her hand and held it tight, waiting. Silence met her before Mark carefully replied, "You don't have to share something so personal, *chérie*...."

Continuing to stare at the tiny book in her hand, she ran her thumb lovingly over it. "I'd like you to know my past before we go any further." Her face creased with lines of anxiety. "This particular notebook is one of my husband's."

Guilt for Mark's earlier actions touched him.

"I would share with you but..." Her voice drifted off.

Curious, he saw the shadow of fear before her eyes. "I carry one myself, as do Mitch and my sister," he offered. When she still said nothing, he added, "Will this tell me something that will change my feelings for you?"

Wilting, she shoved it back into the cabinet, pulling out the oldest book instead. "No. No, it won't. I want to share, I do, Mark, but...will you read this one instead? It shows some things about my husband."

Mark accepted the book, feeling relieved and yet guilty.

Closing the door she paced away from him. "There's another notebook I have...I'll have it mailed to me and get it in a few days. A week most likely."

Mark slipped the book into his pocket. "I do not know what still worries you, *chérie,* but rest assured, my feelings for you won't change."

Leah opened her mouth to reply, intending to confess part of her secret when she saw the message machine flashing. "A message," she said pointing. She couldn't share the book with him.

She had to explain everything first. As she'd held the book in her hand she'd realized that.

She nearly fled to the machine, relieved to have the first part of what could be a very destructive situation over with. At least now he would have time to prepare himself for what she would tell him later.

Mark started toward the door.

Leah hit the button on the machine.

"Hi, Leah, this is Margie. I'm getting everything ready for the new principal here at school and I was going through all the teachers' files. I noted you didn't have any forms from your last school. You told me Philina, right? I can't find anything at all. Someone must have misplaced your file. If you have those could you drop them by the office? Thanks. I'll be here in the mornings. Bye."

Leah clicked off the message, her mind on a new worry. Her records. Oh, dear.

Turning quickly she smiled at Mark. "Sorry about that," she said, though she wasn't. How would she have told him, "By the way, I used to live in Zachary, Louisiana, just a hop, skip and a jump from where you lived in Baton Rouge and if you go back a few years you'll find out just why I'm so wary of police officers"? Crossing the room to the front door where he stood she paused, caught her breath and then said, "I guess I'll see you tomorrow?'' Tomorrow she could tell him...confess at least that she now went by her maiden name.

Mark smiled. ''Wild horses, as they say...''

Relief flooded her. ''Good.'' She'd tell him tomorrow.

Lifting his eyebrows, his eyes twinkling, he said, ''I like the sound of that.'' Leaning forward he placed a gentle kiss to her forehead. ''Until tomorrow.''

He slipped through the door and down the stairs disappearing into the shadows of the trees. When he opened his Jeep's door, she saw a brief flash of him and then his engine started and he was gone.

Leah closed and locked the door before leaning against it. Slumping, she simply allowed the door to be her support. ''Father, what do I do now? He has the first book...but...the one that I want him to have, the one You encouraged me to give him will probably take a week to get here from where I used to live. He's going to be hurt at the least, and furious at the most. Will it matter? Will he care when I tell him? Will he be able to overlook it?''

Reaching up she ran both hands through her hair. ''I don't know what the key is!'' she cried, agitation building. ''What was it in that book that my husband was trying to say? If I could figure out that part then I could at least have something when I face Mark.''

Taking a deep breath she forced herself to relax. ''Help me, Father.''

Standing there with her head bowed she paused and then thanked her Heavenly Father for His goodness and mercy. She refused to leave that spot until she once again had peace and could admit God was in control.

It was a long time before she went to bed that night.

Chapter Fifteen

"That's right, Laura, now cut Thunder to the right."

Mark stood next to the fence where Zach was working with Laura and Thunder, another horse Zach was teaching Laura to rope with. "That's right, easy now..." he encouraged.

Mark watched Laura twirl the rope above her head and then bingo, she let it loose.

The rope sailed easily forward until it slipped around the calf's neck.

Thunder immediately pulled back, digging in while Laura dismounted and rushed to the calf. In seconds it was over, three out of four of the bawling calf's legs were tied.

"Very good," Mark said grinning. "Tell me again why you didn't use your horse?" he teased.

Laura stuck her tongue out at her brother just before releasing the calf's legs.

Zach chuckled. "Jingle Bells isn't trained in this."

"Is he trained in anything?" Mark countered.

"You've got a point there," Zach said. "We'll finish later, honey. I think you need a break."

Laura wiped an arm across her brow and nodded. "Thanks again for working with me. You were right, this is a good workout." Coming over she pecked Zach on the cheek and then grabbed her horse by the reins and walked off.

"She sure is in good shape considering how she just had a baby," Mark murmured.

"I can't keep her down," Zach said good-naturedly. "She wants to learn all kinds of things."

Mark nodded. "Laura always was the adventurous type."

Zach climbed over the wooden fence, dropping down next to Mark. Wiping a hand across his forehead he reseated his hat. "So, what brings you out here today? A visit to your sister?"

Zach's tone told Mark he knew better. Zach was astute, seeming to always know when Mark wanted to talk. Probably came from having two younger brothers whom he practically raised.

"Tell me, Zach, were you ever...interested in Laura's past?"

A look of disbelief crossed Zach's face before he burst into chuckles. "Considering she had my name—and nothing else—in her pocket when I met her, yeah, I'd say I was."

Mark flushed. "Well, yeah. But I meant after you knew her, after well…you two were engaged."

Zach motioned to Mark and then strolled over to the huge maple tree where chairs and a table were located under its widespread branches. Seating himself in the iron rocker he waited until Mark was also seated before asking, "Wanna tell me what's up?"

Glancing out across the broad expanse of emptiness Mark debated how much to share with Zach.

"You can tell me anything, Mark, as long as it's not illegal."

Hearing that, Mark admitted Zach was like a big brother to him, one he'd never had, one he appreciated. "I really enjoy your brother's friendship. Mitch is the best friend a guy can have. He's good-natured, loves to talk and cares—really cares."

"Sometimes it helps to get an opinion from someone you aren't so close to," Zach said mildly, crossing an ankle over his knee.

"Yeah," Mark finally admitted. "And you being Laura's husband and all, I thought you might be able to help me in an area that…well let's just say I have a feeling I'd know Mitch's answer on this. I would rather someone not as close to the situation hear it and give me their opinion."

Silence fell except for the sound of the mockingbirds and blue jays. A wind whipped up the branches of the tree, providing relief to the rising temperature. Laura had disappeared into the barn and hadn't come out yet.

"I called the New Orleans police department to find out just what Laura used to do." Zach answered the original question as if knowing why Mark had asked.

"You did? Why?" Mark asked, glancing at Zach.

Zach shifted his huge frame and then crossed his hands over his stomach. "I couldn't believe Laura would really want to leave there and marry me. I wanted to prove it to her, that there was more there."

"She never mentioned it," Mark said.

"Probably because of the way she looked at it. As far as she was concerned, if I was curious I might as well make sure I had it all out of me before we married. Seeing how matter-of-fact she was when I confronted her made me realize how wrong I was."

Mark scuffed the dirt in front of him with his

boot before saying into the quietness, "Leah's past bothers her."

Zach pushed the rocker moving it slightly, causing it to creak.

"She was married before. That isn't to go any further, however," Mark added quickly. Slipping the toothpick out of his mouth, he leaned forward and turned toward Zach. "I thought maybe if I contacted her last school, someone to talk with, to find out just what happened to her husband—maybe the local police there even—it might help me understand more of her, the pain of her past."

Zach squinted up toward the sky, his thoughts indiscernible. "Maybe."

"You don't think so?"

Again Zach sat for a minute before finally glancing toward the barn where Laura was just exiting. "You know the schoolteacher better than me. She's a sweet little thing but very standoffish."

"That's just a put-on," Mark interrupted. "I think when she lost her husband, who was a police officer, it was in the line of duty. That's probably why she's so wary around other officers."

"I see."

Laura, who had started heading toward them, hesitated, then turned toward the house. Mark silently thanked her for her discretion.

"She gave me her husband's logbook to read.

It's got a few things about duties and such, what I've read so far. I guess I just want to find out more, more than paper can tell me, more than I can ask Leah right now.''

Zach rocked the iron chair again as he crossed his ankles. ''Well, Mark, you certainly have the means at work. Mitch would probably run a routine check for you if you mentioned this....''

''But I don't want anyone else really knowing about it,'' Mark finally admitted.

''I doubt Mitch would mind you doing it yourself. As long as you don't contact these people through official channels since you're on a leave of absence. Invoke the sheriff's name and he'll want to know about it.''

''Yeah. I hadn't planned that, however.''

''What you need to be asking yourself, Mark, is why this is so important to you. Why do you need to know so badly about her past?''

Mark slipped the toothpick back in his mouth. ''I want to help her over the pain.''

Zach finally turned his gaze to meet Mark's. ''Why?''

The squeaking of the front door gave Mark the perfect excuse to glance away. ''We're dating,'' he finally said, ''and I just want to help her get into the real world again.''

Zach sighed. ''Better look deeper than that,

Mark. Be honest with yourself. There's more to it than that or you'd just ask her about her past.''

Disgusted, Mark said, ''Fine. I care about this lady and she just seems…seems…too good to be real.''

Zach chuckled softly. ''There you go.'' Laura, tray in hand with lemonade on it, was headed their way. Zach stood. ''Love isn't an easy thing. Go do what you think is right, Mark. I think you've already made up your mind. You're intent on having the schoolteacher. You're going to make sure she's right for you and that you can't find any reason to push her away. A suggestion, though. Talk to her. A marriage or even a simple relationship can't work without communication.''

Mark stood, tossed the toothpick to the ground and whispered so his approaching sister couldn't hear, ''That's not it at all. I care for her, but that's it.''

Zach lifted an eyebrow in disbelief then chuckled. ''If you say so, Mark. Course, I used to say the same thing about Laura, until she wore me down.''

''What did you used to say about me?'' Laura asked setting the tray on the small table and then pulling a chair over next to them.

Zach reseated himself smiling, ''That you're the stubbornnest woman this side of the Rio Grande.''

"And I've worn you down on that?" she asked pertly.

He grinned. "I let you think so."

Mark simply shook his head. "I gotta go, Sis. You two have fun arguing."

"So soon? But it's Saturday," she protested.

Mark waved a hand. "I have work to do."

"Let me know what you find out, Mark," Zach said and then turned back to his wife, renewing their friendly argument.

Married well over two years now, they still acted like newlyweds. They couldn't take their eyes off each other.

Well, at least Zach had helped him, Mark thought as he climbed into his Jeep. He had been wanting to know just how Leah's husband had died. He didn't feel he could ask Leah. That was not something to ask a wife of a police officer. And besides, something kept niggling at him about the explanation. Why didn't Leah want to discuss it?

She acted as if she were over it for the most part, except for her wariness of police officers. She was willing to share all of her late husband's books with Mark but she didn't want to talk about it. Not really. She said she wanted to talk to him in a week. Maybe that was it. Maybe the foreboding of the way she'd presented it made him brace for something—something that he couldn't understand. By researching her husband, he'd be ready for whatever she had to say.

Evidently, from reading the book, her husband had been a detective. He'd worked several areas. Philina must be a small town from the way his commentary read. The street names sounded familiar somehow, though....

Her husband had been a concise man, recording comments on everything. He definitely kept better data than his father had. Mark had seen his dad's book one time and had tried for hours to decide just what he'd done from reading it.

It had been nothing like this. He didn't understand a few symbols that marked certain entries but many people who kept such notebooks had their own codes they wrote in, their own shorthand. He guessed the reoccurring shorthand in this book referred to some case he and his partner might have been working on at the time.

The more he read the notes, though, the more he wanted to find out about this man. Who had he been?

Driving down the highway toward town, he asked himself if Robert had been a good husband. Maybe he had abused Leah. Had he spent all his hours away like Leah said, or had she exaggerated? He wanted to believe her simply because that's how his father had been. Is that how he'd been killed? Working overtime perhaps.

In the line of duty? Or some freak accident like a drunk driver hitting his car?

He knew if he mentioned it to Mitch, his boss wouldn't think twice about punching in the information and finding out what he could. For some reason, that bothered Mark. He didn't want people to think he was checking up on Leah—especially Mitch or Laura. Yet he wanted that information.

To hear that Zach actually called where Laura had worked stunned him. She hadn't been upset, however. That was his sister, she was always unpredictable.

He thought again of approaching Leah about her past and decided he'd let her tell him in her own time. In the meantime, he'd make a few calls so that he'd be ready when she confessed to whatever it was that bothered her so.

He'd been up most of last night wondering what he was going to do about his feelings. He cared too much for her to ignore them. And if he wasn't mistaken, she cared for him, too.

He couldn't just walk away.

How had his emotions gotten so tied up in this woman? A few weeks and he suddenly found himself thinking of happily-ever-after? Preposterous.

Yet, it was the truth.

If she had healed from her husband's death, if she could really consider having a police officer in her life again, he was actually considering pursuing this…this…

Who was he kidding, he was planning to pursue it anyway and just pray things worked out right. Could he give up police work if he found out she couldn't be involved with another officer?

He thought about it and didn't really have a pat answer. He had wondered about his career choice most of his life. Could he simply walk away or was it in his blood? Somehow, he had the feeling he was going to find out for certain with this woman. God had a way of forcing people to face their fears or past hurts and conquer them. He was afraid this was the road he was now at or fast approaching. A time of growing, as his sister would call it.

Turning down Main Street he waved to everyone he saw before reaching the sheriff's office.

After killing the engine, he climbed out of the Jeep.

He nodded to the dispatcher as he headed down the hall. He knew that the equipment in Mitch's office would help him locate Leah's past. He also knew no one there would stop him, and that Mitch wouldn't mind him using his private lair for a short time to do the computer search and calls.

As long as he did it unofficially. Once in Mitch's office he pushed the door closed and went to his desk.

After seating himself, he pulled up the national directory on Mitch's computer. Pausing with his hands poised over the keys, Mark tried to remember the name of the elementary school mentioned on the answering machine. "Philina."

That was it...though something once again touched his memory that he couldn't quite name.... Typing in the name of the city, it was only a moment before he had the number of the police station. Pulling out a small notepad, he wrote it down and then compiled a list of information he knew on Leah.

Husband: Robert Hawkins, dead at least four years—the time she has been teaching here. No more than ten years, considering Leah's age.

Work: Detective, more than likely a small town.

Putting the end of the pencil to his mouth, he considered what else he knew that might be useful. Schoolteacher.

A few more scribbles, and he was done.

Snagging the phone, he placed it between his shoulder and ear and quickly dialed the number listed in the directory.

He wrote down the name of the police department and then waited until the dispatcher picked up on the other end. "Ah, yes," Mark began, wondering if he sounded as stupid as he felt. "My name is Mark Walker from the Hill Creek, Texas Sheriff's Department and I'm calling about a former police officer there named Robert Hawkins. You see—"

His hand paused in writing. "He wasn't? It would have been most likely four years ago or longer. Were you there then?" he asked.

At the answer from the other end, he frowned. "Twenty years, huh? Just what size of town are you?"

Scratching down the information, he added the figure for the town's population, twelve thousand. "Uh-huh…"

The memory that had been bothering him returned, telling him he was missing something. The missing link ate at him as he listened to the woman go on and on about the Philina Police Department. "Maybe then you might know about a schoolteacher, Leah Thomas?"

Writing down Leah's name he paused when the woman told him no. "Elementary teacher most likely, not the high school or— Still no, huh?"

Frustrated he decided he must have heard wrong or— "Okay, thank you very much, Officer Jenkins."

He hung up the phone finally honing in on what

had bothered him. Turning again to the computer, he pulled up Philadelphia's police directory. He remembered now in an earlier conversation, Leah had mentioned Philadelphia to Mitch. It was entirely possible Leah had simply lived in Philina or taught there after her husband's death.

After finding the numbers for the Philadelphia Police Department he wrote them down, realizing this was going to take a while. Turning to a fresh sheet of paper, he began writing and calling.

Chapter Sixteen

Church was already in progress when Mark slipped in the door to the foyer. He felt as if he hadn't slept in three days, and worse.

Pulling at his shirt again he quietly crept through the lobby and pulled open the back door to the main area of the church.

Pastor Ferguson was preaching. Several kids in the back row turned to see who had come in, most likely expecting a friend. Sherri, Freckles's sister, sat with the group. Her eyes perked up with both reproof and then interest at seeing him.

It didn't matter which emotion she showed, he flushed anyway. He was nearly forty minutes past due for church.

Glancing around, he located his sister and her

husband and the rest of the gang up front and to the right.

No way was he going up there.

Then he spotted Mitch, in uniform in the back row without Suzi. She must be working in the nursery, he thought, since Mitch was on call today.

Mitch saw him and motioned him over, scooting to make room.

With a last quick glance at the teenagers on the right, including Sherri who had made room for him, he nodded a quick greeting and headed left toward Mitch.

Going to the far side he slipped into the pew and seated himself. As he did, he caught Leah's eye. She had turned just as he'd seated himself. She sat up front with Freckles and Hawk.

Mark waved, thinking about going up there and then deciding it would be too much of an interruption for those around them. He settled in next to Mitch.

Leah nodded, her eyes showing how happy she was to see him, then returned her attention to Jon's message.

"Oversleep?" Mitch whispered quietly.

Mark winced. "I'll explain it all after church."

Mitch nodded.

Mark turned his gaze to the front and worked to pay attention to what Jon had to say.

As much as he tried, he couldn't get his mind off last night. Which was a shame since Jon had a good message. Mark caught the gist of it. Sometimes we have to believe more what God tells our heart than what we see. Faith. Pure and simple. When God tells us it's going to be all right, then we can bank on it.

Mark wished that was the case here, he mused as Jon continued to expound on how we could apply this to our daily lives. The pastor also explained how we were at war with the flesh.

He knew all about warring in the flesh. As he'd searched last night for the information on Leah and her husband, his mind had hammered over and over that he should just forget the search. His flesh said he liked her, and nothing else mattered. His flesh told him to go to her and find out what was going on and then bury it if it was something he didn't want to know.

His heart told him otherwise. The more he searched, the more worried he became. He wasn't sure why. Perhaps it was that inner instinct Mitch said he had, but something wasn't right. Things about Leah didn't add up.

His alarm bells were demanding he pay attention. She was a schoolteacher yet her records were incomplete and there had been no Leah Thomas registered as a teacher in the last five years any-where in Philadelphia. Not that he could find.

But he knew Leah.

Glancing to where she was, he thought she couldn't be deceptive. She was too sweet, too gentle, too—Leah!

Why had he even started looking in the first place?

That cop instinct in him was demanding he pursue this, that something wasn't right. The rest of him was demanding he ignore it and just be glad Leah was going to explain everything—whatever it was—in a few days.

This was all just a mistake.

Again, for what seemed like the one thousand and oneth time, Mark said a silent prayer: *Show me what is going on here. Help me understand so I can comfort her. So I can be comforted, too, with the missing information.*

"Hey, bud."

An elbow to his ribs drew his attention to Mitch.

"Church is over. So, before you go tearing off here to speak with Leah, why don't you tell me what's up?"

Indeed, Mark noticed the people just turning and breaking up. He realized he'd missed the altar call and the final prayer, he had been so preoccupied.

So much for going to church, he thought, disgusted. He'd been totally absorbed.

"You were late." Leah spoke the words softly, smiling at Mark as she squeezed through the crowds.

All worry fled at the touch of her gentle warmth. "I overslept," he repeated.

"I tried to call."

Mark's heart thudded. "I didn't even hear if Freckles or Hawk knocked." He flushed a bit at admitting that.

A person squeezing by in the aisle jostled him, bringing his mind back to why he'd overslept and he sobered.

"Were you coming over for dinner today? I thought we could finish the plans on the outing. I got papers today, the final approval on the pictures we took."

Mark opened his mouth, not sure how he was going to reply when Mitch broke in. "I'm afraid I'm going to need him for an hour or two today, Leah. I'll send him over afterward."

Mark saw the wariness flash in her eyes before she allowed her disappointment to show. That was what caused the foreboding, he realized. Anything to do with Mitch or police work caused a look that shouldn't be there. It wasn't pain, but wariness.

His heart clutched.

Was she still married and lying to him? Was he afraid of finding that out?

"I'll see you later, then?"

Mark nodded. Hesitating, he finally leaned down and planted a gentle kiss on her forehead. "Promise."

Her cheeks turned pink and her eyes warmed, melting the ice in his heart. "Okay." With a quick smile at Mitch, Leah headed out of the church, a Bible clutched in her hand. Before she could leave, Mark saw Tessa waylay her and was glad. Perhaps Tessa would invite her over for dinner, and she wouldn't be left alone....

"I really do need your help." Mitch nudged him then slipping his hat on, he headed out a side door.

"Oh?" Mark asked and followed Mitch out of the church.

Mitch headed down the sidewalk toward the office. Mark followed, leaving his Jeep parked in the street. "What's up?"

"Wanna tell me why I have a ton of information on my desk, all to do with Philadelphia?"

Mark ran a hand down his face. He started to fish for a toothpick, but changed his mind and left them in his pocket. "Leah."

One word, uttered so simply but somehow he felt he was betraying her—betraying her and he didn't know about what, why or how. But he was, just as sure as he knew his name.

"What about her?"

Mark rubbed the back of his neck before following Mitch into the sheriff's department. "That's what I need to explain."

He nodded to the dispatcher, Carolyne, and headed on down the hall, quietly following Mitch.

Once in the office, with the door closed, Mark started pacing. Mitch didn't seat himself but leaned against the desk, watching. He could feel Mark's tension.

Trying to appear nonchalant, Mark said, "I told you a bit about Leah and what was going on...."

When he hesitated, Mitch nodded. "Go on."

Mark swiveled and threw his hands in the air. "I wanted to check up on her, Mitch, find out what had happened to her husband, just what she might be going to tell me tomorrow or the next day... whenever she said she was going to tell me—"

"Whoa." Mitch lifted a hand. "Slow down, Mark. You're losing me here."

Mark sighed and dropped down onto a chair. Unable to resist, he pulled out a toothpick, his salvation in the matter, his way of forcing himself to concentrate and stay calm. "Leah told me she had something to tell me. Whatever it is, it's got her shaken. I assumed it was about her husband. I know he died—I think..."

Shaking his head in self-disgust, he added, "Of course, he's dead. Mitch. I've checked Philina where she evidently taught. At least that's what the school said. When I dropped her home the other night there was a message on the answering machine saying they needed her school records from Philina, records that she'd never had transferred. But she told you she'd taught in Philadelphia. Come to find out, the two are a good three hours away from each other. And she isn't or hasn't been either place at all."

"Okay, Mark, let's take this from the beginning."

Mitch moved around his desk. Sitting, he pulled out a tablet of paper and a pen. "Just what do think Leah might be covering up?"

"Nothing," Mark snapped, offended at Mitch's words.

Mitch held up a hand. "Hold on there, Mark." Rubbing a hand over his lip, he studied Mark. Finally he lay the pencil down. "Listen to me a minute, Mark. I want you to pretend you're the police officer and I'm offering you information."

Mark knew where this was headed and didn't like it.

Mitch waved a hand. "You're too agitated,"

Mitch warned. "Listen to what you're saying from my point of view."

Mark started to object and then nodded. Maybe Mitch could put this all into perspective, and then he could apologize to Leah.

"I just got some information on a new person in town, hypothetically speaking. The person was hired but has no background records when I checked the file. The two places I have heard her mention have no record of her working there. She's wary of police officers—"

"But—" Mark started.

"Ah—" Mitch warned.

Mark subsided.

"She keeps to herself. If this was anyone but Leah, tell me what conclusions you would draw?"

Mark scowled.

"You have just told me these things," Mitch continued. "Now, I have two questions for you."

Mark nodded.

"Judging from how you both greeted each other in church, you two haven't had a fight. Correct?"

Mark nodded and slouched.

"I know you're not making up the facts but... well..."

Mitch shifted uncomfortably.

"Just say it, Mitch," Mark demanded.

"You haven't been drinking?"

"I don't drink," Mark said, disgust in his voice. "You know that."

Mitch nodded. "Then could this all simply be circumstantial?"

Mark could see Mitch felt the same way he did. "I can't imagine her having done anything. But if that's so, why can't I find any information on her? It's like she just dropped here in Hill Creek."

"You realize, Mark, that you can't get rid of those instincts in you?" Mitch said mildly as he turned to his computer.

"You're telling me. I was here until 3:00 a.m. trying to find information on Leah's husband. The more I looked, the more frustrated I got."

Mitch clicked on his computer and typed in his password. Pulling up his menu, he said, "Let me propose a few ideas."

After Mitch pulled up the screen he wanted, he then turned back to his notepad. He started writing as he talked. "You're worried about Leah. Something more than this has triggered your fear. It could be legit, or it could be simply you didn't think you'd ever marry and are trying to find a way out."

"I don't want out. I just want to know if…"

"Yes?" Mitch asked, pausing over the pad.

Mark sighed. "I just want to know if she could consider marrying another police officer."

Silence reigned in the office for nearly an eternity before Mitch said softly, "Then I won't be looking for a replacement for you?"

Mark threw up a hand. "How can I leave?" Scowling, he pulled the toothpick out of his mouth, and tossed it in the trash.

Mitch chuckled.

"Leah has helped me realize, however inadvertently, that my heart is with this job. I enjoy what she and I have done, but I have missed this. I found the real reason I have enjoyed being out in the wild was simply because Leah was at my side. But, in finding that out, I realized I...care...deeply...for her."

"And she was married to a man who died in the line of duty."

Mark shrugged. "I do not know. That is what I wish to find."

Mitch motioned at his pocket.

Mark scowled again and pulled another toothpick out and jammed it in between his teeth.

"You get too stressed, bro, and I can't understand you. Now, go on."

"I don't know how to approach Leah. I don't know about her husband. She wants to tell me something but asked me to wait until this week and then she would. I suppose I've been imagining all kinds of things—"

"Including that she might still be married?"

Mark grinned sheepishly. "Well, I can't find anything on her or her husband."

Mitch went back to writing on the pad. "Did you consider the following? One, she was married a second time for a short time and divorced and she has a new name. Two, that she may not be going by her married name. Three, that if you want to really find out about her, and you're that worried, check out the crime lists and work your way back."

Mark sighed. "I was going simply on the teaching and police officer angle."

"I have a couple of ideas. But first, why didn't you come to me and ask if you wanted to find something out?"

Mark's cheeks flushed with heat. Quietly he admitted, "I didn't want you to think I was checking up on Leah."

Mitch shrugged. "You are only doing what I would do if I'd thought Suzi had been married and had a husband who had been a police officer."

"I was also not sure how Leah would see it."

"Now there you have a point." Mitch paused at his computer and glanced at Mark. "I'll be glad to check up for you, but when Leah tells you whatever it is we find out, I want your promise that you'll let her know you did this and explain why."

Mark nodded. "I had planned to." He paused. "Maybe I shouldn't look it up after all. Maybe I should have just gone to her and asked her to tell me whatever it was."

"That would have been the way," Mitch agreed. "But sometimes that's hard. Tell you what. Since you're here, let me go through official channels and see what I can find out. Give me thirty minutes. Or until a call comes in." Mitch grinned and Mark knew it was because a call on a Sunday afternoon was very unlikely.

Mark nodded. "I do want to know."

Relaxing back in the chair, he said quietly, "You should see her, Mitch. I'm not sure how her husband died, but it still bothers her. I don't know what to do. When she is hurting, it hurts me. The other night in the barn she cried her eyes out over something that bothered her. All I could do was hold her."

Thinking back to how he felt, he added, "I wanted to shout my frustration over the fact I couldn't take away the hurt."

"She's a sweet gal," Mitch murmured as he started accessing files.

Mark smiled. "Yeah. You know, after what had gone on in my family I could never imagine myself as a family man, but with Leah—you know, I can actually see us having kids and settling down."

"Hey, that's God there. I don't think any man can truly imagine that until God gets hold of him."

Mark chuckled with Mitch. "I don't mind giving up my bachelorhood. I had worried that by marrying someone I'd eventually have my dad's life, but you know, watching you and Suzi, watching my sister and Zach..." Mark shook his head. "I guess I was seeing through the eyes of hurt and anger instead of reality."

Mitch nodded. "We tend to see through our parents' eyes. Don't forget, Mark, that you choose how your life will be. You can choose to spend time away from your family or you can choose to sacrifice in some areas to make sure you have family time."

"I've been thinking about that a lot."

"A few months ago do you remember the sermon the pastor spoke on? He talked about Christ being the head of the church and the bride being the body of believers? If you look at marriage like that, Mark, look at it as you are representing Christ's love when you marry your wife and your wife is representing the church...."

Mark nodded. "Yeah. Christ gave up his life for whoever would be part of that bride."

"An awesome responsibility, bro," Mitch replied and then frowned.

"What is it?"

"I found a Leah Thomas here that is our Leah Thomas's age. Actually I found several."

Mark nodded. "Good."

Mitch started making notes as he continued to talk. "I've found with Suzi that we both have to compromise. She and I can lock horns, but we've learned a lot from Jon about just what our marriage should be. If you love Leah and she loves you, just remember what Jon said…it'll take work. But it'll be worth it."

Mark nodded. "I don't see how it could be any other way."

"None in Philadelphia. Hey, here is one that was born in Louisiana," Mitch said, changing the subject.

Mark chuckled. "How about that."

"Let me do another quick check here."

Mark stood and walked to the bulletin board to study the different announcements and pictures up there. "I guess she's going by her maiden name maybe?" Mark asked.

"Possibly." As Mark waited, his thoughts drifted to everything he and Leah had gone through since they had started working together on her project. It was thirty minutes and five calls later before Mitch called out, "Found something."

Mark, who had ended up leaning against the

wall, pushed away and strolled back over to the desk. "What's that?"

"Police officer that married a Leah Thomas."

Mark dropped into a chair next to Mitch. "Oh, yeah? That's gotta be her. That's it!" Mark leaned forward. "I know what it is that's been bothering me now."

"Oh?" Mitch asked.

Reaching for the logbook he started flipping through it. "Here, and—" he flipped through several more pages "—here. The French-sounding streets. Two of 'em. That's what was bothering me. Why didn't she tell me she was from Louisiana?"

Mitch frowned. "Maybe because..."

Mark sighed. "Because her husband died there."

"Tell you what, why don't you go get us both some coffee and lunch and I'll have some more information when you get back?"

"Sounds good." Mark sighed. "I appreciate this, Mitch," Mark said and headed out the office.

By the time he returned from across the street with lunch and coffee, Mitch had indeed found something.

Setting the two plates down, Mark walked up to where Mitch stood by the fax, staring at a paper. "What'd you discover?"

Mitch looked up, the muscles in his face tight, the look in his eyes...

Mark's stomach dipped at that look.

It reminded him of an expression he'd seen on his dad's face the day his mom had died. One that brought bad news. Really bad news.

"What is it?" Mark asked.

Mutely, Mitch held out a paper.

Snatching it with a shaking hand Mark turned it to read—and when he did, his entire world fell apart.

Chapter Seventeen

"**I**'m serious, Leah. The man who called had your looks down nearly perfect except he was looking for a Leah Hawkins."

Leah was certain she was going to be sick. Staring at Margie who sat at the table with Tessa and her husband and Frank, all teachers from school, she couldn't think of a reply.

Her worst nightmare had resurfaced. "When was this?" she managed to ask.

"Friday. I started to call but was so swamped with getting all of the other paperwork in line that I totally forgot. He said it was a school reunion. I'm surprised he hasn't contacted you yet."

"You gave him my number?" Leah said this calmly. All of those around the luncheon table had slowly grown quiet. She prayed they didn't notice her anxiety. She prayed but knew it was useless. They all watched out for her in this town. Anything out of the ordinary would have everyone asking questions of her.

"I told him you were in the phone book."

"Ah," Leah said and smiled.

She smiled though her mind raced.

She had to get out, escape. They had caught up with her. What would she do? Mutely, she sat there trying to hack out a plan.

When she didn't say anything else, Tessa leaned over and kissed her husband on the cheek. "I'll clear the dishes and then we can all play Scrabble. Good for Drake's dexterity." Tessa winked at her, but Leah couldn't smile.

Drake gave his wife a patient loving smile as she stood.

Leah's heart nearly broke.

Mark!

In her rush to escape the coming events she had not thought what she would say to Mark.

What was she going to tell him?

"I'll help," Leah said and stood. She started gathering the plates.

"I hope I didn't say something wrong," the red-haired secretary said, worriedly.

Leah shook her head. "No."

"Why don't we go into the other room?" Drake suggested, standing.

Frank pulled out Margie's chair and they all headed into the living room.

Leah took her load of dishes into the kitchen, intent on only one thing. Escape. But could she escape from Tessa? She knew Tessa. Her friend wouldn't simply let her walk out without an explanation.

Leah didn't have long to wait for Tessa to follow her with her worry. She was right behind, trailing her into the kitchen through the swinging door.

"Are you okay?"

Leah flipped on the water and started rinsing the plates for the dishwasher. "I'm fine. Really."

"I know you better than that, Leah," Tessa said quietly.

Tessa started loading the dishwasher.

"I really need to go home and make some calls. I hope you don't mind if I leave early."

Tessa paused in loading. Glancing at Leah, she studied her. "The person who called shook you up, Leah. Someone from your past?"

Leah paled thinking how true that was. "Yes. Things I don't want to remember. I'm expecting some mail today or tomorrow—express. I really should be at my house just in case it comes."

Leah wasn't lying. She'd asked her friend who

worked at the school system in Philina to forward
the book to her. She'd gotten a call saying she'd
mailed it yesterday. But that wasn't the only reason
she wanted to go home.

She had plans to make and things to do. And if
she knew the person who was after her, she had
no time in which to do it. Her time could already
be up.

Tessa hesitated then straightened from the dishwasher. "I'll tell you what, Leah. Why don't you
go on home and wait for that package? I'll call
Mark and have him go over there."

"No...I mean, well, I'll call Mark instead." At
a time like this, Leah didn't want their worry. Nib-
bling her lip she reached out and caught Tessa's
hand. Squeezing it, she said softly, "You're the
best friend I've always wanted, Tessa, and I appreciate it, but I just really need quiet time. I'll call
Mark, when I'm ready. Please, don't worry."

Tessa wrinkled her nose in disagreement but
nodded. "I can't help but worry. However, I'll
give you your quiet time."

Relieved, Leah smiled. "Thank you."

"Go get your purse. I'll finish up here."

"Thank you, Tessa," Leah said and hurried out
of the room. She passed the living room and went
down the hall into the room where she'd tossed her
purse earlier, the entire time thinking about Mark.

What was she going to tell Mark?

Had she run out of time?

Why couldn't this have waited just a few more days?

She'd have been ready then. She was going to tell Mark everything, confess all the secrets she had kept up until now.

The past kept searching for her, hadn't given up.

Pausing in the bedroom she worked hard to hold back her tears. "Why now, God?" Wiping a hand across her eyes, she whispered, "If I had done it when You'd first told me to, I'd still have time, wouldn't I? Why did he have to find out where I am now? I don't want Mark to hear about me from anyone but me. I have to tell him."

Taking a deep shuddering breath she told herself to just stay together a short time more. She could cry when she got home. Then she'd call Mark. No, she'd go to the sheriff's station to tell him. That would be best.

"Why, God? Why does this have to happen now?"

She realized the way her legs trembled that she was actually terrified. In that instant she had to ask herself if she really would have gone through with it. Would she have actually told Mark everything if her hand hadn't been forced?

She had been having trouble sleeping since she

had decided to tell him. She had kept wondering what to tell him and how....

"You're forcing my hand," she whispered. In a way she was thankful that God had allowed it all to come to a head like this. She had no choice now. The secret she had kept so long would have to come out.

Of course, that terror of facing Mark, of seeing his face was still there.

How would he react?

There was only one way to find out.

Leah turned and headed out the bedroom and down the hall, intending to tell everyone goodbye and go straight to the sheriff's office instead of home.

She was surprised when every eye turned toward her.

And even more surprised when she glanced around to see the sudden interest in her stemmed from the two people who stood just inside the front door.

When she met Mark's gaze she knew.

She knew her secret was no longer a secret.

The story was told in his eyes. The cold empty look where love had been pierced her through.

"I—" she began, and realized her mouth was so dry she couldn't speak.

Her one word galvanized Mitch. He started forward. "Leah, honey, can we talk out—"

Mark's hand shot out.

Surprised, Mitch glanced at him.

Please, God, her mind screamed while her body stood frozen. She couldn't have moved if her life depended on it. Her legs were turning to jelly even as she stood there.

"Leah Thomas-*Hawkins*. You're under arrest for the murder of Robert Hawkins—your husband."

At Mark's words, the entire household erupted into noise.

Margie cried out in shock. "Murder?"

Frank lunged to his feet. "What!"

Tessa started toward her. "You're crazy! What did you say?"

Drake stood up to forestall his wife. "Explain this!"

Mitch said something that she had never before heard come out of his mouth.

And Mark. Mark's gaze had turned from cold and empty to burning with betrayal and hurt. Coming forward he reached for her hand.

The cold metal of a handcuff snapped on, sending another round of shouts and outrage through the house.

"That's not necessary, Mark," Mitch said coming up.

"It is," Mark returned, his gaze not leaving Leah's.

"No. It's not. Nor was this scene," Mitch growled.

Shouldering his way in, he reached for Leah's hand.

"Mark—" she whispered.

Mark shook his head, then with one long last look, he turned his back on her.

As his back turned, the entire world faded to Leah. With one cry of dismay she gave in to the overwhelming shock and pain and sank into merciful blackness.

Chapter Eighteen

"You could have waited until we were outside."

Mark stood staring at the wall in the police station. His entire world continued to spin out of control as he listened to Mitch's diatribe.

"She deserved more than that."

"She's a liar and a murderer," Mark said flatly.

Mark swung around under Mitch's grip as the bigger man grabbed him by the shirt. "You haven't heard her side and you are already accusing her of being a murderer."

Mark shoved an arm toward the desk where the Wanted statement lay. "That says it all. What more can she say?"

Mitch glared at him in silence.

Mark shuddered, his anger breaking as bleakness filled him. "Tell me, Mitch, what more can she say?"

Mitch released Mark and glanced toward the door that led back to the cells, the area that Mark realized held Leah and Freckles, who had come to check her out.

Finally he glanced back at Mark and sighed. "I called the sheriff in Zachary. Someone is already on the way from the East Baton Rouge Police Department. But we could have at least asked her what her side was before bringing her in, Mark. Which is what I wanted to do, until you confronted her and whipped out a pair of cuffs."

Mark sank into a chair and ran a hand through his hair. "I'd heard of the murder. Word like that gets around. They thought the wife hired someone to kill off her husband. I was making a lot of road trips at that time and did not hear all of it. I'm sure Laura can tell you all about it. Even in New Orleans they will know of a cop killing."

"Do you really believe Leah did that?"

Hearing the note in Mitch's voice he glanced up. Mitch stood towering over him, his gaze curious. "I—"

"Search your heart," Mitch said softly.

Mark did and finally he shook his head. "I know her. I love her. How could she do such a thing?

But as you pointed out, she has hidden so many things.''

"Yeah, but why? The schoolteacher I know isn't like this. I do have some other questions for her, when Freckles is done in there.'' Mitch ran a hand through his hair.

"Another phone call. This one from the school principal, Sheriff. You want to take it?'' Carolyne poked her head in the door.

Mitch glanced at Carolyne and shook his head. "Take messages from them all. No one is to get any official information. Tell Zach, though, I'll call him back in a couple of hours and Laura to come on in and help run interference.''

Carolyne nodded and slipped back out.

"The whole town is going to be over here soon,'' Mitch muttered.

"I want to see her.''

Mark simply stared at the shocked look on Mitch's face. He didn't comment. He imagined his request sounded funny since he'd arrested her.

Mitch hesitated. "I'm not sure I can let you do that,'' he finally said.

Mark was finally regaining his equilibrium and realized that he had to talk to her, to find out the truth. "It's important, Mitch.''

"You're one of my officers. This is an important case.''

"I'm still on leave. Fire me if you have to. I've got to talk to her before anyone else gets here. I have to—I don't know—apologize or something," Mark pleaded.

Mitch hesitated again.

"I love her," he said softly. "I've never begged for anything Mitch, but I'm willing to beg to talk to Leah."

Mitch sighed. He opened his mouth to reply when he saw Freckles returning.

"How is she?" Mitch asked when she stepped into the office.

Freckles, looking a bit shell-shocked herself, shook her head. "Considering she's been accused of murder and everything else that has happened, she's doing well. I gave her a mild sedative. It should help her relax until..."

Mark's heart constricted at Freckles's words. Until the police showed up. "When did they say the officer from Louisiana left?"

Mitch scowled. "Funny thing. He should be here today sometime. Seems like he is driving and left yesterday."

"He's known that long? But how?"

Mitch shook his head. "The permit's in her name for the state project. Evidently this person coming, the dead officer's old partner, has never stopped looking for her. He took it personally that his partner was killed on a bust gone bad—one his wife set up and paid someone to do.''

''I don't believe it,'' Freckles said bluntly. ''Leah couldn't do that. If she had, it was before she committed her life to Christ. She's not that type of person.''

Mitch nodded. ''But if she did, even if she was a Christian, Freckles, we'd still have to bring her to justice.''

Freckles looked as if she wanted to say more—a whole lot more—but she refrained.

''She shouldn't be back there alone,'' she finally said.

Mark looked to Mitch. ''Let me.''

''I thought you arrested her,'' Freckles said.

''I did.''

''Then I don't think—'' Freckles began.

''He loves her,'' Mitch interjected.

''Odd way to show it,'' Freckles said softly with a hint of reproach.

Mark continued to stare at Mitch, his agitation and need to see Leah pushing him to the point where he was about to go through Mitch to get to her if necessary.

Mitch obviously recognized a look of desperation when he saw one. Finally he nodded. ''Okay. But let me remind you—''

''Sheriff?''

Mitch turned toward the door. "Yes, Carolyne?" he asked, exasperated at another interruption.

Mark was, too, until he saw the stranger behind Carolyne.

He had *cop* written all over him. This had to be the man coming for Leah. But how so quickly?

"Dan Milano, sir. He's from Baton Rouge, Louisiana."

If Mark wasn't mistaken, Mitch was rather surprised and bothered by this man's abrupt arrival.

Still he was polite. "Officer Milano," Mitch said and extended a hand.

The man named Dan stepped into the office. "I hear you've picked up a woman named Leah Thomas also known as Leah Hawkins."

"Word travels fast," Mark muttered.

"Not at all. Seems you called the office there and they radioed me. I had hoped to keep it quiet in case word got out, as it does in small towns. Evidently your checking up didn't tip off the assailant."

"Yes, well," Mitch said, "I was about to question her. She was brought in rather abruptly, and we haven't had a chance to talk to her."

"Really?" Dan seemed pleased with that. "Good. She has made quite a trail across the

United States. Pennsylvania for a year, California for all of two months and now Texas. Everywhere I've found traces of her she'd laid down a sob story. We lost track of her in Pennsylvania. Evidently we found she'd gone to California but once again she disappeared.''

"I see. I'd like to wait a day, if you don't mind,'' Mitch said, breaking into Dan's tale of the chase. "I'd like to talk with Leah, but give her a day to rest up. You see, the Leah we know—''

"Afraid we can't wait a day. I promised them I'd be back to work by Monday. I had planned to arrest her today and start back, stopping overnight in Baytown or Orange before going on to Louisiana in the morning.''

"What?'' Mark was astonished and panicked. He wanted to talk to Leah before she left.

Dan glanced at Mark curiously. "Gotta stay under budget with travel arrangements.''

"I'm sure one day wouldn't hurt,'' Mitch said.

Dan shook his head. "It might have been possible if she wasn't in custody and I had to explain everything to you. Now it'd be useless.'' Pulling papers out of his pocket, he handed them to Mitch. "I'll take my prisoner now.''

Mitch stared at the papers. Mark felt the pain and frustration grow.

"I gave her a sedative and really don't think she should be moved," Freckles interjected.

"And you are…?" Dan Milano asked.

"Dr. Susan McCade. It's mild, something for her to relax—"

"Which would really benefit her on the road," Dan interrupted.

Mark saw the look on Mitch's face and knew he had no choice. "I'll get her," Mitch said and turned to leave.

"I'll go with you," Freckles offered, her frown showing her displeasure.

Mark's gaze went back to Dan. When the door had closed and it was only the two of them, Mark said, "I'm deputy sheriff here and made the arrest. Tell me, are you certain she is guilty of this crime?"

He had to ask. He hoped with that bit of information he could get more out of this man.

"No doubt about it."

"How do you know? I mean for certain. Leah…Mrs. Hawkins just has never struck any of us as a violent type."

"She's not, Deputy," Dan said now, his gaze changing to one of sorrow. "She's a very quiet, dainty woman. That's why she hired someone. I found all the information in her house after she had deserted it."

"I don't believe that," Mark argued. "If you only knew Leah…" he began.

"Oh, I know Leah," Dan said, his gaze narrowing. "I used to have dinner with her and her husband and was even there when she announced her pregnancy and—"

"The child whose death you are responsible for!" Leah shouted. "Had I not been running and hiding from you I might have—have—" Leah caught her breath, swallowing emotion.

Mark turned toward the door and saw Leah, in handcuffs, standing there with Freckles holding her on one side and Mitch on the other, his hand at her lower back.

"Leah…" Mark murmured. Seeing her standing there like that… He'd done this to her. How had he allowed this to happen?

His mind cleared. He knew he didn't just care for this woman. He loved her. He would do anything to protect her.

Anything.

But it was too late to tell her that now. He'd arrested her. He could never make it up to her.

Ever.

"He's lying. He's the murderer. Because of him, because I had to go on the run, I miscarried!"

Leah broke into sobs.

Dan glared at her, stepping forward and then

restraining himself. "You had your husband murdered, Leah. You've given us a good chase, but we found you. You knew eventually we would. I loved your husband like a brother. Did you think I'd let you go without tracking you to the ends of the earth?"

"Leah. You didn't do this," Mark said, softly, carefully stepping forward.

Leah pulled back so he couldn't touch her, piercing his heart. "You arrested me. Are you saying now that you didn't have a warrant?"

Mark heard the bitterness and couldn't blame her.

Dan cut a hand through the air. "Enough chat. She will tell her woeful tale to anyone who will listen. You should hear what she told them in Pennsylvania." Shaking his head, he moved forward and took Leah by the arm.

She staggered a bit, obviously from the sedative. She couldn't evade his grip.

"I don't think you should let her go," Freckles said worriedly.

"No choice," Mitch said through stiff lips. "However, I do plan to call the Baton Rouge department and talk to them. I think there's been a mistake."

Dan nodded. "Do that. They'll fill you in. Better

yet, call Zachary and ask them just what went on. Every cop there knows the story.''

''I want to go with her,'' Mark argued.

''Sorry. Something more is going on here with you and her,'' Dan said very astutely. ''I'm not taking you along in the car—especially if I don't know what this felon has been telling you. Come on, let's go. Thank you, officer, for your promptness.''

Dan took Leah by the arm and then quickly started out the office and down the hall.

Leah glanced over her shoulder and on a sob, cried out, ''Mark...''

Mark started after her.

Mitch grabbed him.

''Let me go,'' Mark demanded.

''Not this way,'' Mitch countered.

''I have to,'' Mark said as Leah and Dan disappeared from view. ''You don't understand, *mon ami*, I have to go after her and tell her I love her. I was wrong.''

Mitch shook his head. ''It won't work. Listen to me.'' Gripping Mark, he shook him.

Mark stiffened and raised a fist when he realized what he was doing. Stepping back, he got control.

''Call in favors from friends down there. Go to New Orleans. We can get Laura on it and you have friends. We'll find a way to get to the bottom of all this.''

"She didn't do it.'' Mark knew in his heart, she wasn't guilty. He just knew it. He'd been a fool.

"I know,'' Mitch said. "We'll prove it, or at least help her some way. But we can't break the law and just keep her from this guy,'' Mitch soothed. "Now let's—''

"What's going on? Where's Leah going in that car? Who was that guy?''

Mitch turned. "It's a long story, Laura,'' Mitch began.

"The Hawkins murder in Scotlandville, that tiny town near Zachary, a drug-related murder of that cop a few years back? Remember that?''

Mark said that to his sister who, disheveled but in her uniform had stormed into the office.

"Yeah? What about it? I remember a little bit.''

"She's the wife.''

Laura laughed. "No way.''

Mark nodded bleakly. "Call in favors, Laura. I'm going to Baton Rouge.''

"You're what? Wait a minute!''

He shook his head. "No time. Have people down there willing to talk to me when I arrive. I want to go by Leah's, Mitch, and get her some personal things. Then I'm going to Baton Rouge to try to see what I can do.''

Mitch nodded. "But he worked for the Zachary police."

"Zachary and Scotlandville are both suburbs of Baton Rouge," Mark explained impatiently.

"Ah," Mitch said. Nodding he added, "Good idea." Running a hand through his hair he muttered something Spanish under his breath. "I understand. I hope, for your sake, Mark, you find this is somehow a mistake."

Mark nodded.

"I'll go with you to Leah's house, however. You can't go in there without me. I'm going to have to cordon it off and go through her things."

"Well I'm going now. So, let's go."

Mark headed out the door. Laura stopped him. "Go to Davey's. He'll put you up," she said speaking of one of their lifelong friends.

"I will," Mark said.

"I'll call and let him know you're coming."

Again Mark nodded.

He started out and then paused. "I need your help, Sis. I can't let Leah go to jail. Not until I talk to her. You see—" he paused, his gaze blurring "—I'm going to marry her—one way or another."

Laura bit her lip, pain mirrored in her eyes, then she kissed his cheek. "Go."

And he did, leaving the office and heading to

his house. He then stopped by Leah's house and picked up whatever he thought she might need while they were in their hometown of Baton Rouge.

Chapter Nineteen

"Where are Bobby's books, Leah?"

Leah sat on the couch at her house, staring mutely ahead.

"I'm not going to ask you again. I've followed you all over and I know you took some things out of your house, some of Bobby's things as well as stuff that hit man gave you. Where did you stash them?"

"Why should I tell you?" she finally muttered, working hard to shake off the lethargy the drug in her system had caused.

She should be terrified, but instead, everything seemed far-off, as if in a dream. Why, oh why, had she let Freckles give her the drug? She should have told Mitch and Mark what she had but her mind—

it just hadn't been working right. It still wasn't working right.

"You have to tell me, Leah, because that's evidence and you wouldn't want to tack on more charges."

That nasty voice of his chilled her. "You killed my baby."

Dan paced over to her, jerked her up and leaned into her face. "You ran. It's your own fault."

Leah's heart contracted over the long-ago pain of loss.

"We don't have all day. I stopped here to get the information. You said it was here. Where?"

"You're going to kill me, aren't you?"

Dan's hand tightened on her arm, his nails digging into it as he jostled her.

She winced and tried to jerk free but stumbled.

"What does it matter? That'd be better than a life on the run, wouldn't it?"

"I lied," she replied.

Dan paused for a moment staring at her in utter shock. "You lied? About the information? What do you take me for? A fool?"

Leah twisted her hands, cuffed so securely in front of her. "If you believe I have the information on me, then yes, I take you for a fool."

Dan studied her a moment more before backhanding her.

With a gasp, she fell backward against the sofa.

"You wouldn't have enough sense to hide the information," he growled. "Bobby said you were an innocent, too naive to ever understand what he did on the side. You wouldn't know to do something like that."

The sharp slap that split her lip had the good side effect of clearing her senses.

Looking up in pain, she said softly, "I may have been innocent in many ways, but I wasn't naive— or at least I learned not to be, Dan. You taught me that."

Dan let loose with a string of curses that caused Leah to wince again.

"You and that husband of yours. Christianity!"

He laughed harshly and pulled his gun from his shoulder holster. "That just proves how weak you were. Christianity is for the weak-minded, for the weak-stomached. That was the problem with Bobby. Do you know he had actually rededicated his life to *Christ* and wanted to become more of a family man? He got a conscience. He would have eventually spilled the information the way he was headed. It's not that surprising I had to clean up the mess he'd made by deciding to go all goody-goody."

Leah realized this man planned to kill her. He never would have confessed to her husband's death otherwise. With a silent prayer she sent a plea up to God to help her.

Glancing furtively around, she tried to think of a way to escape. Dan paced back and forth as Leah pulled herself up straighter on the sofa. Slowly she stood.

"He was a fool. He was going to give it all up. I couldn't trust the man. Any fool who would believe in a God that you can't see, someone who supposedly has your best interests at heart and makes you suffer, couldn't be trusted to keep his mouth shut."

Swinging around, he came forward and pulled Leah to him. Waving the gun at her, he glared. "Now," he said steely-soft. "I want to know where that information is."

"In another state," Leah said simply. She had a peace she couldn't believe that she would have had at this point. Maybe it was because she realized God was in control. Just as with Elijah when he'd faced the many priests or Jezebel who'd wanted him dead, she knew God would see her through this.

He shook her, her head snapping back in pain. "Tell me the truth. Where's the account book your husband kept of the drug transactions? I have to have that destroyed before I can kill you, too."

The front door slammed open just as the back door swung inward.

Leah gaped, shocked to see an enraged Mark heading in the back door. She wasted no time, but grabbed at Dan's collar as he jerked her toward him for protection. Instead of fighting, she went with him, slipping a leg behind him and knocking him to the ground.

Though she tumbled with him, she kept rolling toward where Mark stood.

Dan roared in outrage. Mitch started across the room toward Dan, but he wasn't fast enough. Dan jerked his gun out and aimed.

"No!" Mark shouted and lunged at Leah.

The gun went off.

Mitch returned fire almost immediately. The bullet hit the fireplace as Dan rushed Leah.

Mark shoved Leah to the ground as Dan lifted his gun, aiming again.

"No, Mark!" she cried, grabbing at him as pure fear raced through her veins.

She was going to lose him. Dan was going to kill the second man that had come into her life. It wasn't fair. Her gaze focused on the ever present toothpick gripped between his clenched teeth as Mark pushed himself back so that he could take aim and fire. Jerking the tiny piece of wood with all of her strength, she acted on pure instinct and lunged toward Dan shoving the weapon at his face.

Dan lunged back, off balance.

It was enough of a distraction that Mitch grabbed him by the shoulder and shoved him down—hard, to the floor.

Dan screamed again and reached for them, his gun coming up.

Mitch's knee went to the back of his neck and he jerked the gun away.

They grappled.

Mitch slammed his arm down on the detective's neck. "Don't move," he shouted.

Dan wouldn't give up, though.

Mark turned, his face full of pain, and grabbed the man by the hair, holding him. That was enough for Mitch to whip out the cuffs and secure him.

Mark collapsed.

Leah, gasping for breath, scooted forward on her knees. Cupping his cheeks with her manacled hands, she couldn't help but sob. "Don't die, Mark," she whispered.

Mark groaned. "Shoulder wound. I'll be okay, I think."

Following his gaze to the bloody sleeve, she examined it. "It tore the skin. Oh, Mark, it looks awful."

"It's a mild wound. Don't worry."

"You stay put. I'll call for an ambulance and get this guy to the station. You, Leah, are still under arrest until we get this all straightened out."

Leah nodded.

"I'll leave her in your custody, Mark. After what little we heard, I think she'll be cleared."

He hauled the bleeding and bruised Dan out of the house calling over his shoulder, "I'll be right back as soon as backup arrives." Leah could hear him talking on the small radio to dispatch.

"You saved my life," Leah whispered when it had finally grown quiet. Ripping at his sleeve she laid some of it over the wound to staunch the bleeding.

"I saved *our* life, Leah," Mark said.

"But you thought I was guilty."

Mark shook his head. "I was a fool. I arrested you out of hurt. I had been struggling with whether or not to remain a police officer. When I got that information I was so angry I wanted to prove something. I'm so sorry, Leah. All I proved was I love you and I'd willingly give up everything to have you as my wife."

Stunned, Leah sat back.

Mark winced. "I didn't mean for it to come out that way."

"But—but you don't know what I did," Leah whispered.

"Tell me," Mark said. He moved forward and painfully settled next to the blood-covered Leah, thinking they both looked like survivors from a minor war. Touching her puffy lip and slightly bruised face, he waited for her to tell the story she needed to explain.

"I married young, Mark," she said. "I loved Bobby, as I had told you, but we'd grown apart. I was going to church, Robert had stopped until a revival meeting. He changed, though, and I could tell something was bothering him. I wasn't sure what. The day he died, a young man showed up at my door. He had papers that my husband had given him and said to get to me. He said it was awful and he had to get out of town, but that my husband had saved his life and wanted me to have them. He wouldn't tell me anything else. I knew, though, from the look in his eyes, I knew my husband was dead."

Leah shuddered. "I didn't accept it, though. I opened the papers and saw his notebooks. One I gave you. Another had a code in it. The one I am waiting on—"

"That is here now," Mitch said, walking back in, a postal official by his side.

"Uh, sign here?" the young man asked looking from one person to another in question.

"Go ahead," Mitch said to the man. "Leah can sign."

She did and then ripped open the overnight box and tipped it upside down. Mark caught the book and handed it to Mitch. "That book and the accompanying paper talks about meetings in Scotlandville, meetings that have to do with drugs. At first I couldn't figure it out, but as things started coming out about cases Bobby was working on, I figured out from the book it was drugs.

"I realized at his funeral that Dan had to be in on it. Dan was in all of these meetings."

Mark glanced to Mitch for confirmation. "Yeah. Looks like meetings all right and bookkeeping records of some sort."

"They didn't coincide with his official book, the one you have, Mark. This was a separate one. I packed up and left. Dan was hot on my trail. Evidently, he'd taken a leave of absence to hunt me down. He caught up with me in Philadelphia."

Mark pulled her into his arms and hugged her. "I'm so sorry," he whispered.

Leah shuddered. "I had gone to work in Philadelphia, you see. A friend in Philina wrote me a recommendation—under my maiden name. I have no full records under my maiden name, only under my married name. The old principal here, being so easygoing and understanding that I was worried about a person from my past, had agreed to keep my file separate. He allowed me to work under my maiden name." Sighing, she ran a hand through her hair. "This was all such a mess. The new principal wanted my records. It was all going to come out so I was going to tell you."

"But Dan found out."

"I guess. I wanted to tell you, Mark. But how could I say I was wanted for murder? I found that out when I called a friend back in Zachary and she told me. I cut all ties after that day."

She broke into fresh sobs. "How can you even stand to look at me after all that?"

Mitch cleared his throat. "I think the ambulance is here—as is Freckles," he muttered and headed toward the door. "She turns up everywhere, it seems."

Mark waved him off and continued to hold Leah. "It doesn't matter. You're not guilty. Listen to me, Leah. I love you. I was a fool to worry over silly things. Who cares about the past? Who cares about what you or I do as a job? None of that matters. The only thing...and I mean it...the only thing that matters is God brought us together. You healed my heart when I thought it was beyond healing. God opened my eyes to what is important.

"Mitch will get this all cleared up. And all I

want, Leah mine, is to hold you. To love you and to grow old and fat together. How about you?''

Leah squeezed Mark.

He tried not to wince. ''All I want, Mark,'' she whispered through her tears, ''is you, a husband to hold, for the rest of my life. Do you think we can do it?''

Mark whispered back, ''Do you think Jesus can forgive us of our sins?''

''Always.''

''Then, yes. If He can do that, can die for us, nothing else is insurmountable.''

Leaning back she met his gaze. ''I love you, Mark.''

''And I love you,'' he replied and leaned down to kiss her.

Epilogue

❧

"**Y**ou sure you're ready?" Mark asked, offering his arm to Leah in their unorthodox wedding. After all, when did the groom escort the bride down the aisle?

Leah straightened her long ivory wedding gown, touching the pink flowers in her hair before nodding. As she laid a hand on Mark's arm that wasn't in the sling, she felt a bulge in his tuxedo jacket. The bone in his arm had ended up chipped, and he'd had to keep it in a sling for six weeks. But this wasn't pain medicine she felt.

Mark reached for the container in his pocket.

Leah grabbed it instead. She held it up to him, grinning while they waited for their music to start on the organ. In the six weeks since Dan had been arrested, information had come out that proved Leah innocent and Dan guilty. All charges had been dropped. Mark, finally deciding what he wanted, hadn't wasted any time. He'd gone back to work for Mitch, gotten Leah's agreement for a quick wedding and with the help of friends, planned it all in three weeks. "I guess I didn't need your lessons for guns after all, a toothpick did just as well."

Mark chuckled. "You saved both of our lives with that. To think, I had that toothpick in my mouth because I didn't think my French accent fit into this part of the country."

Leah leaned forward. "If you don't mind, I'd rather have a French-talking cowboy as a husband. I sorta like the accent," she said flirtatiously, having opened up and blossomed before him in the last three weeks in a way he'd never expected to see.

"Oh, yeah?" he asked now, grinning wickedly at her.

She nodded, her smile mirroring his. "Oh, yeah."

With a silly grin he tossed the toothpicks into a bush by the front door of the church.

Mitch, Zach, Drake and Julian stood by the altar as witnesses. Also present on the opposite side were their wives. The church was full as the flower girls began walking down the aisle. Kristina and two other children from Leah's class tossed pink rose petals.

"I can't believe they've all forgiven me for my deception."

"They love you. Tessa is taking the class on the trek for you. Mitch spoke before the board of directors and got you reinstated and you and I are getting married. What else can you ask for? Or not believe?" he quipped.

"You mean other than the house on Mrs. Culpepper's property that she is letting us have?"

Mark glanced to where the former Mrs. Culpepper, now Mrs. Whitefeather, sat. The two had eloped just a week ago and offered part of her land as a wedding gift to Mark and Leah.

"Well, yeah," Mark said grinning.

Leah glanced up, all the love she had shining in her eyes. "Only that you promised to be my husband to hold the rest of my days."

Mark smiled and leaned down, giving her a soft kiss. "You promise me the same."

The music for the bride's walk started.

He turned to the door, Leah's arm tucked in his elbow. "And since a promise is a promise..."

He stepped forward, Leah at his side.

The two made their walk down the aisle with most of Hill Creek, Texas, watching. And on that day they pledged their love as a covenant before God, promising to live from that day on, in love and commitment, so help them God.

* * * * *

Dear Reader,

We all struggle with the question: what do we do now? In this story both Leah and Mark struggle with this question. Mark, haunted by his past, can't decide what to do, and Leah, hiding from her past, is afraid to step out and decide what to do. However, when love happens, God brings them both to a place where they must make choices.

I know I've faced that in my own life, and I know many of you have and some of my younger readers will. And by the way, thank you to the many, many, *many* readers—both male and female—who have written, from age eleven to age eighty-seven, thanking me for the books. When I make decisions about writing a book, I remember the many things you've said and it's an encouragement. Blessings to you all. I hope you enjoy this one!

Cheryl Wolverton

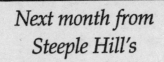

*Each month
you can find three
enchanting new stories from
the leader of inspirational romance—*

Love Inspired®

More than heartwarming tales of inspirational
romance, these original stories celebrate the
triumph over life's trials and tribulations
with an editorial integrity you can trust.

Featuring new releases each month by the
world's most respected authors, Love Inspired
is the name you count on most for value,
convenience and above all else, integrity.

Available at fine retailers near you.

Steeple
Hill™

Get caught
reading
Love
Inspired.

Next month
from Steeple Hill's

Love Inspired

HEAVEN SENT
by
Jillian Hart

*Successful photographer Hope Ashton comes home to
Montana to care for her grandmother and encounters old
flame Matthew Shaw, a widower raising triplet sons. Soon
Matthew's mother and Hope's grandmother are hatching a
plan to bring them together. With lives as different as day
and night, will they discover that their love for God and
each other can bring them together?*

**Don't miss
HEAVEN SENT
On sale July 2001**

Love Inspired

Visit us at www.steeplehill.com

LIHS